MEET ME AT
Sunrise

MEET ME AT
Sunrise

A Romano Family romance

Lucinda Whitney

Lange House Press

Edited by Michele Holmes and Haley Swan
Cover design © 2018 Lange House Press
Layout and Formatting by LJP Creative
Published by Lange House Press

First Printing May 2017

ISBN 13: 978-1-944137-23-6
ISBN 10: 1-944137-23-8

\

Quem tem família, tem um porto seguro.

One who has family has a safe port.

Romano Family

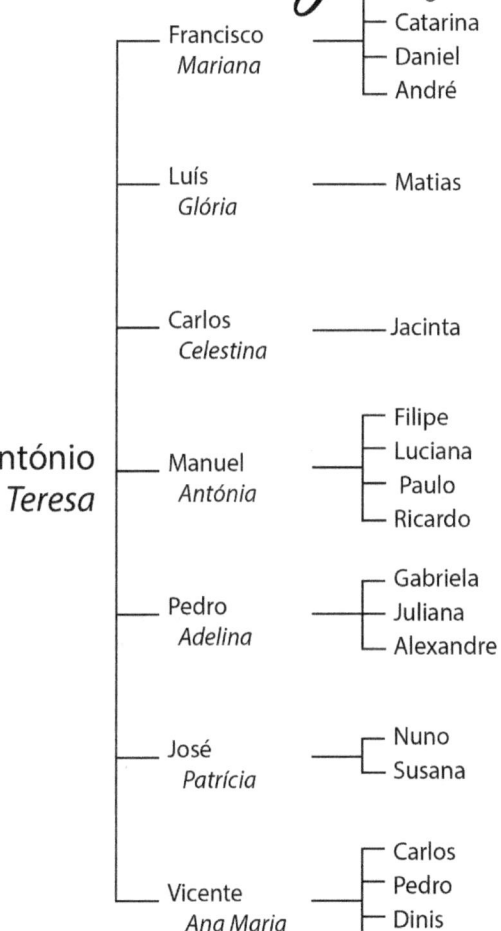

António
Teresa

- Francisco
  Mariana
  - Tiago
  - Catarina
  - Daniel
  - André

- Luís
  Glória
  - Matias

- Carlos
  Celestina
  - Jacinta

- Manuel
  Antónia
  - Filipe
  - Luciana
  - Paulo
  - Ricardo

- Pedro
  Adelina
  - Gabriela
  - Juliana
  - Alexandre

- José
  Patrícia
  - Nuno
  - Susana

- Vicente
  Ana Maria
  - Carlos
  - Pedro
  - Dinis
  - Anita

CHAPTER ONE

*T*his was a bad idea. Why had she let Grandfather talk her into this trip?

Vanessa stopped at the entrance of the ship's formal dining room and gazed around. Outside the panoramic windows, the city of Porto inched up the hill from the docks on the other side of the river, the buildings and roofs and church towers competing for space unsuccessfully. Myriad lights shone against the night sky and spilled in reflective ribbons on the water's surface. In its architectural disorganization, there was a beauty that called to her. It was a city so unlike the ones she was used to. Much of Portugal was still a mystery to her.

Inside, the passengers sat in groups of eight at round tables, and waiters in white coats flitted between them with silver platters and bottles of wine. Everything in the room spoke of elegance and luxury,

1

from the furniture and dark wood trim to the impeccably white tablecloths and fresh-cut flowers to the damask draperies drawn back with silver ropes and the pianist undulating at the baby grand.

She'd barely looked at the pamphlets Grandfather had sent her and was not prepared for the real-life opulence before her. She—the Kansas girl who preferred well-worn jeans and flip-flops to dresses and high heels—aboard the *MS Princess Catarina,* the crown jewel in Grandfather's fleet of luxury river ships. How long until someone recognized she didn't belong here?

A very bad idea indeed.

At least she was by herself. She'd managed to convince Grandfather she didn't need the bodyguard he'd planned to send with her. As president of a multi-million-dollar company, he was the one who needed bodyguards. She was just an American girl on her own, and nobody knew of her yet. Besides, what could possibly go wrong on a small cruise ship?

Inside her clutch, her phone rang. It was probably Dad. Again. He'd insisted on being able to contact her throughout the trip and had prearranged a new plan with Verizon. He'd have to wait until tomorrow to talk to her.

An appetizing scent reached her nose. Roasted pork, rosemary potatoes, and something else she couldn't identify. Vanessa was late to dinner and she had missed the "Welcome Aboard" cocktail party. The light breakfast from this morning was only a memory by now. Her stomach rumbled.

The maître d' appeared at her elbow. "May I have your name, please?"

Vanessa turned to him, grateful that English was the official language aboard. "Vanessa Clark. Is it open seating?" she asked, while he checked the list in front of him.

"Not for you, Miss Clark. Please follow me."

As he cut a path to the center of the dining room, Vanessa ignored the urge to smooth her dress and held on to her sequined clutch instead, carefully stepping on the gleaming wood floor and willing herself not to trip on her strappy sandals.

Was it her imagination or did most people pause to look at her? The conversations and clinking of silverware against the porcelain dishes continued on around them, as a few of the passengers darted their eyes at her. This was karma for being the last one to arrive at dinner. For someone who didn't like attention, she sure had a lot of it now.

The maître d' pulled out a chair next to a dark-haired man in a black uniform. He was clean-shaven and appeared to be in his early thirties, with an air of confidence that drew her attention. Who was he and what did he do?

The man stood and nodded at her. "Good evening, Miss Clark."

Her eyes widened for a moment. How did he know who she was?

He didn't smile openly, but his mouth curved into a pleasant expression, and Vanessa's lips rose in response.

"I'm glad you made it." His voice was deep and lightly accented, and his arresting brown eyes held hers for a moment longer than good manners called for.

After an awkward pause, they sat down and Vanessa dragged the bib-size napkin onto her lap, looking away from him and realizing the other guests at the table were staring at her. She drew a quick breath. There was a spotlight directly above, and the heat from it bore a hole in her head. Was the air conditioning even on? Goodness, he was just a man, and not even the most attractive one she'd ever met. Why the sudden discomfort?

"Is this your lovely wife, Captain?" The lady across from them asked.

Captain? Wife? Vanessa turned to the man, noting for the first time the white stripes on his sleeves. "I'm sorry, I didn't realize you were the captain." Her cheeks heated at the mistake. She was seated to the captain's right, without a doubt arranged by Grandfather.

He cleared his throat. "She is lovely but no, not my wife." He shrugged in a self-deprecating manner, and the other passengers at the table chuckled lightly.

He turned to her. "I'm Captain Romano, Miss Clark." He then addressed the other passengers who shared their table. "Allow me to introduce Miss Clark, from the United States of America." He started at his left and went around the table. "Dr. and Mrs. Whitehead, from the UK; Mr. and Mrs. Grantham, also from the UK; and Mr. and Mrs. Grosse, from Germany."

Vanessa nodded and smiled politely at them before they returned to their meals.

"Miss Clark, I apologize for the blunder," one of the English ladies said. "But there was an empty chair next to the captain and he seemed to have been waiting for you." She looked between Vanessa and Captain Romano. "And you two make such a striking couple."

Vanessa's cheeks reddened, the curse of a light complexion, courtesy of Dad's Scandinavian ancestry.

"I haven't had the pleasure of meeting Miss Clark until now," the captain said.

Vanessa nodded. "Yes, what he said." She cringed inside. Why couldn't she come up with an appropriate reply when she needed one?

She busied herself with the perfectly seasoned potatoes on her plate instead. If she nodded and looked interested in the conversations around her, maybe she wouldn't have to say too much and could save herself from any more embarrassing responses.

"What state are you from, Miss Clark?" the German man asked, his accent evidence of his origins.

Vanessa paused to look at him. "I'm from Kansas."

His forehead wrinkled and he looked at his wife who gave him a small shrug.

"It's in the middle of the country. You know, lots of farming and fields, *The Wizard of Oz* and tornadoes," she explained, her words running together.

They nodded in understanding. Maybe she should stop talking now.

Vanessa waited for more questions, but thankfully none came, and she slowly let out a small breath of relief as the attention shifted from her.

One of the English men put his fork down. "Captain Romano, is Chef Teresa still on your crew?"

The captain smiled. "She certainly is. In fact, I have the same exact crew as last year." The pride in his voice was unmistakable.

Was this a common occurrence, to ask after the crew? Her knowledge of cruise etiquette was ridiculously poor despite what she'd read before coming, and even though Grandfather owned the vessel.

The questions continued for the rest of the meal, keeping the captain busy as he gave everyone his attention. How did he find the time to eat? His patience was admirable.

As the courses changed, the captain picked up the bottle of red wine, and Vanessa watched him pour a glass of the burgundy liquid for her. She thanked him and brought the glass to her lips, tasting a drop too small to swallow. The flavor was foreign to her, and she chased it down with a large gulp of the mineral water from the other tall glass in front of her. As she set the glass down, her hand trembled, and she tightened her grip on the stem until the base touched the table. How much longer until she could take refuge in her cabin?

As another waiter slipped a plate with the next course in front of her, she looked casually to the neighboring tables.

Couples. All the passengers sitting in the dining room were couples. Middle-aged and senior couples eating and talking and laughing. She couldn't find another person close to her age among the hundred and thirty passengers. The growing uneasiness tightened in her chest, and she suppressed a sigh. What had Grandfather done, sticking her on a fancy river cruise with the upper crust of Europe?

Captain Romano leaned in her direction. "Is everything all right, Miss Clark?"

Vanessa's tongue stuck to her palate, and she took another drink of the barely cold water. "Please, call me Vanessa, Captain." She raised her eyes to him. "Have you met my grandfather?"

One of the waiters came to the captain and handed him a small card. He tucked it in his pocket and then turned to the rest of the table. "Excuse me, ladies and gentlemen. I am needed elsewhere for a moment."

As he stood, he made eye contact with Vanessa. "Excuse me, Miss Clark," he said to her.

Vanessa nodded in response, not knowing what else to say. Why did he single her out?

What an unfortunate time for him to leave, and how disappointing for her. Now she'd have to wait for another chance to ask him about Grandfather.

Matias Romano looked around for the cruise director. When he spotted her across the room chatting with a group of passengers, he rose and excused himself from the last table. He always took the time to greet all the passengers after dinner and he wouldn't start making exceptions on this trip. But he could leave the rest of the evening in Anabela Rialto's capable hands. Mingling and interacting with the passengers were some of her duties, and Matias had observed over the last few trips and she seemed to enjoy that part of her job.

He had other matters to think about. Like Miss Vanessa Clark. They hadn't had a chance to talk in private at the table, and she had left the dining room abruptly after the dessert course was cleared, not even waiting for the after-dinner espresso to be served. If she had returned to her cabin, he'd have to talk to her some other time. But leaving her question unanswered wasn't ideal, and he felt obligated to set a friendly tone between them.

He quickly exited through the main lobby and climbed the stairs to the sun deck. He stopped short before reaching the bridge. There she was, to the starboard side, leaning casually by the railing, looking out to the city on the other side of the river. Her face was in profile, and her long blonde hair blew gently in the breeze. It was a lovely scene and she was a lovely woman, but there was nothing more to it.

So what if he was partial to blondes? A pretty face didn't hold much interest for him when she'd behaved so snobbishly at dinner. She had picked at her food and barely spoken to any of the other passengers, gazing around the room with an air of aloofness instead. As the only granddaughter of the company's president, she was probably used to the royal treatment, but that didn't give her the right to look down on the other passengers. Suddenly, talking to her wasn't a pressing matter anymore.

Why had he agreed to António Valadares's hare-brained idea? Sure, he could hardly deny any request from the president of the entire fleet of river cruise ships, but acting as a personal guide to his heiress granddaughter was not in Matias's job description. He should have said no, plain and simple. He was the captain, not a babysitter to a young woman who had everything. But his sense of duty had prevailed instead, as it usually did. There was more at stake than his personal preferences. Senhor Valadares had hinted at a problem with the future of the company, but Matias wasn't sure how it tied to the granddaughter.

Matias slowed down and squared his shoulders, letting out a slow breath. A hint of anticipation flared up, and he quickly squelched it, annoyed with himself at the twinge of attraction that sparked for a second too long. He only needed to talk to her. Nothing more.

She stood barefoot, her high-heeled sandals lying on their sides, her small purse next to them. Matias resisted the urge to return them to her and shoved his hands in his pants' pockets. He cleared his throat to greet her, but she spoke first.

"How many times have you made this trip, Captain?"

"Quite a few, Miss Clark." He faced the city as she did.

This was his seventeenth time up the river on this particular route. He knew because he'd been recording all his trips—not only the cruises but also the fishing and stocking ones—since he'd boarded his first boat as a deck hand at the age of fourteen. There were official records as well but he didn't like admitting to that level of precision and mostly kept the exact number to himself. "Miss Clark—"

She interrupted him. "And just how long have you been working for this company?"

Matias turned to her. "Is there a reason to your questioning, Miss Clark?" He kept his tone level and even, but his fingers tightened around the key ring inside his right pocket. What was it about this woman? He'd barely met her, and already she set him on edge in a way no one else had in his recent memory.

She leaned away from the railing and turned partially to him. "Just trying to determine how well you know my grandfather."

"Yes, you asked me that earlier. I'm sorry I didn't reply." They'd been interrupted by another passenger needing help, as he was so often during meals.

Matias took a quick breath and braced himself
for more questions. He didn't know what to expect
from her and it made him uneasy. The reaction was
new to him, but she was more than a simple passenger, and it would serve him well not to forget the
connections she had. "I have met your grandfather
on several occasions since I started working at the
company."

She turned away from him and let out a long sigh.
"Probably more times than I have." Her words came
out quick and low, and maybe not intended for him
to hear.

"Is there a problem?" He paused and made eye
contact.

"Not a problem exactly." She looked away and
drummed her fingers along the rail.

"Is there something you're not happy with, Miss
Clark?" They hadn't even departed, and already she
had complaints. Usually he left the passenger-related
matters to his cruise director, but not this one. She
was in his hands, whether he liked it or not. "I know
you're probably used to more personal service, but
if you give us a chance, you might be pleasantly
surprised."

Miss Clark's eyebrows knit in a scowl, but she didn't
comment right away. After a long moment, she asked,
"Are all the cabins as large as mine?"

"Excuse me?"

"The cabin assigned to me. Is that the standard
cabin size?" She fidgeted with a length of hair, and

when his eyes turned to it, she dropped it and flicked it behind her back.

The gesture lasted only a few seconds, but he lost his train of thought as it latched onto the woman in front of him. Matias struggled to resume their strange conversation. "Actually," he shook his head. "Uh, no. Your cabin is one of two deluxe cabins on the ship. We refer to them as the grand cabins, and they're reserved for our VIP passengers."

It was her turn to shake her head. "He did it, didn't he? He put me in that cabin?"

This conversation was turning more bizarre each minute. "If there's a problem with your cabin, I'll ask Miss Rialto to look into it. She's our cruise director, and I'll introduce you if you haven't had the chance to meet her. Your grandfather requested you stay in that particular cabin since it's the largest and best on the ship, and I have an obligation—"

Her eyes went wide. "Obligation? Obligation to what?"

Not to what, to whom. Her, to be exact. Matias didn't reply.

"To me, isn't it? You were going to say you have an obligation to me, weren't you?"

Matias flinched at her words and the way she'd read his mind. He rubbed his forehead. "It's not like how you make it sound." He forced his eyes to her. "Yes, I have an obligation toward you but it's the obligation I have toward all the passengers on board as well as my crew. I am the captain, after all."

Her shoulders relaxed a fraction, and Matias pressed on. "Your grandfather only wanted to make sure you have the best experience on this trip and even you can't fault him for that." Matias knew from his own research that she was his only granddaughter.

"I'm sure he did." She shook her head lightly, and her shoulders slumped even more, as if something weighed on her. "I don't need a babysitter, Captain. In case you haven't noticed, I'm a grown woman."

He'd noticed all right. More than he wished to, but he wouldn't be telling her that.

"Did he tell you why he wanted me to take this trip?" she asked.

Matias fumbled to find a reply and she waved him off. "That's okay, I don't want to know what he said. There's enough drama as it is."

It was family drama and he should stay out it. Well, most of it. He was already involved.

After a moment, she straightened and met his eyes. "At what time does the boat leave tomorrow?"

"The ship departs after lunch." He emphasized the word to correct her. It certainly wasn't a boat. "There's a guided excursion in the morning."

She bent to pick up her shoes and tucked the purse under her arm. "What are the rules about leaving?"

"Any time the ship is docked, you can leave at your leisure. But if you don't make it back before departure, we can't hold it for you."

She nodded. "That's only fair."

As she walked past him, he cleared his throat. "Nobody will prevent you from leaving if that's what you wish to do, but I hope you'll consider staying, Miss Clark." He wanted her to stay, and not just because the company's president had asked him. Proving to her that the trip was one worth taking had become more important than he'd anticipated.

Before she reached the staircase, he called after her. "Miss Clark."

She stopped and looked over her shoulder.

"Please be careful when you come out on the sun deck." He looked down at her bare feet, and she followed his gaze. "Oftentimes the floor is wet and it's easy to slip. I wouldn't want you to get hurt."

She pivoted, raising her fingers in a mock salute. "Aye, aye, Captain."

CHAPTER TWO

*T*he sun wasn't up yet when Matias arrived at the bridge. He greeted his first mate and nodded at the deckhand. "Good morning."

"*Bom dia, Capitão,*" the young man replied.

"You know the rule, Pedro. English only." Matias enunciated the words slowly and clearly. The young man's English wasn't perfect, but it wouldn't get any better if he didn't use it more.

Pedro's cheeks heated. "Yes, Captain." He put down the tray with two coffee mugs and breakfast croissants, then left.

"You could go easy on him," Miguel said from his chair.

"I could, but then it would take him longer to learn the language." English was the official language for a good reason. With so many international passengers, it was easier to set the expectation that everyone speak one common language than trying to accommodate individual needs. The expectation fell onto the crew as well.

Matias looked out the window. A thick fog hid the river and the banks under its gray layers. Some of the passengers would be surprised, but he had seen fog occur at any time of the year, regardless of the warm temperatures the day before. It would dissipate as they traveled up the river, as it usually did. He reached for the day's newspaper.

Something gray and solid moved ahead on the prow and he squinted. "Who's that out there?"

Miguel looked up from his place at the small desk. "That would be the special passenger." He turned back to checking the weather predictions on the iPad.

Matias's forehead wrinkled as he tried to distinguish who the figure was.

"You know, the one you've been asked to keep an eye on." Miguel kept his head down, unusually tempering his normal curiosity.

"That's Miss Clark out there?" Matias whacked the newspaper against the nearest counter, his voice unable to hide the annoyance and surprise at seeing her outside his window this early in the morning.

He yanked at the door and walked outside the bridge, rounding the prow to where she stood. For a moment, he thought he'd find her perched on the railing, à-la-*Titanic*-movie, but she was firmly planted on deck and wearing appropriate shoes. He let out a breath, the relief filling his chest and putting a stop to the adrenaline that had shot through his system a minute earlier.

The woman was throwing off his balance, and he hadn't even left the dock. He hadn't slept well, thinking about her and their exchange of words the night before, unable to get her out of his mind. What was he going to do about her?

She glanced at him. "Good morning, Captain."

Her cheeks and nose were red, and the top of her jacket covered the bottom half of her face up to her bottom lip. The hood flopped over her forehead, effectively hiding her long blonde hair. She looked younger than her early twenties, more vulnerable and insecure. The contradiction to the extremely put-together woman he'd met last night was more than what he could deal with at the moment, and he pushed the curiosity away.

Matias nodded at her, then turned to the bridge and knocked at the glass to get Miguel's attention. He pointed at the coffee carafe, and Miguel poured a cup and met him halfway.

Matias touched her arm, and when she turned toward him, he held the cup in front of her until she took it.

She rested the cup against the railing and pulled the zipper down with her left hand to uncover her mouth. Then she sipped quietly, both hands wrapped around the mug, her eyes closed in soft appreciation.

"What are you doing out here at five o'clock in the morning, Miss Clark?"

"I wanted to see the sunrise, Captain Romano." Her breath came out in little puffs, and her voice held a small tremble.

"That's not going to happen today." His words sounded harsher than he intended and he cringed inside.

Miss Clark raised an eyebrow at him over the rim of the cup and kept sipping.

He softened his voice. "I mean, the sun will rise, of course, but we won't be able to see it through the fog." Before he lost the gumption, he continued. "Listen, Miss Clark. I wanted to apologize for my gruff words last night."

She lowered the cup and adjusted her fingers around it. "I do too, Captain." She kept her eyes down on the dark liquid for a moment, then raised them to him. "I mean, apologize. I was angry at my grandfather, and I shouldn't have taken it out on you."

Anger? There was more to the story between António Valadares and his granddaughter than what Matias knew, and he probably should keep it that way.

"And I shouldn't have reacted so poorly. I'm sorry." The tightness in his chest eased a bit as he voiced the apology. He always kept his behavior professional toward his passengers, and he would treat her the same way.

Miss Clark's expression relaxed, and her eyes locked on his. She was taller than most women he knew, and the short distance between them put her nearly to eye level with him. She had green eyes framed by long light-brown eyelashes, and a few freckles dotted her skin on the bridge of her nose. No make-up this morning. Just delicate, creamy skin and eyes the color of the river on a winter day.

For a moment, a prick of interest niggled at him. What was she like in her day-to-day life? What did she do for fun? And why was she on this trip when she obviously hadn't chosen to come?

He occasionally wondered about a passenger on a personal level, but only in passing and seldom with the intent to truly know more. But this situation was different. His questions went beyond superficial interest this time.

It didn't help that she was young and attractive, and it had been a long time since Matias had given himself permission to think about a woman and the possibility of going out on a date. Fortunately, he had enough responsibilities to keep him physically busy and emotionally unavailable.

If only his thoughts were as easy to direct.

Vanessa looked away from Captain Romano's chocolate-colored eyes.

What had just happened? Yesterday they'd been short and almost rude with each other, and now, after offering apologies, something had passed between them: something warm, zingy, and unexpected. Something totally unrelated to the coffee in her hands.

19

He took a step back and she did the same. Good. More distance between them was what she needed. Standing near the broad-shouldered captain with the deep brown eyes and the sexy voice muddled her thoughts. She had to get away from him and clear her head.

Vanessa tipped the cup and drank the rest of the coffee the captain had brought her earlier, most likely from his own pot.

"Was this your coffee?" She held the cup to him and he took it.

"We keep a carafe well filled."

She slipped her hands into the kangaroo pocket of her jacket. "Thank you for sharing. I underestimated the weather this morning."

"You're welcome. And you're not the only passenger who didn't expect to see fog in the summer."

They stood in silence for a minute, watching the rolling wisps of gray as if they'd part to reveal the city on the other side. Vanessa peered at the captain, but, just like the fog that hid everything around them, his face disclosed nothing of his thoughts.

A tap sounded on the window, and they turned to see the other crewman motioning to the phone. Captain Romano nodded back at him.

"It looks like you're needed." Vanessa tipped her head toward the bridge.

"After you." He gestured for her to walk ahead of him. "By the way, good choice on footwear."

Vanessa stood there for a moment as he entered the bridge, a faltering smile on her face at the unexpected comment.

When she arrived at her cabin, she fell back on the wide bed and kicked off her shoes. They weren't exactly traditional deck shoes but more of a crossbreed, with a ballerina-flat shape and solid rubber soles. No slipping on the sun deck in these babies. And they were red, which she loved.

Even better, Captain Romano approved of her choice. It shouldn't matter that he did, but the happy feeling inside her wouldn't abate, even when she tried to force it to go. After a short moment, she gave up the fight. When was the last time a man complimented her? Nothing came to mind. She'd had a few dates in college, but the compliments had seldom sounded sincere. Compared to the captain, those guys had only been overgrown boys who mostly wanted one thing from her. Captain Romano was older, but there was something about him that went beyond age and maturity: something intriguing and attractive.

She shook her head. It was pathetic. *She* was pathetic. A man had offered her a compliment and there she went setting him up as the yardstick of perfection by which all other males had to be measured. Had she been like this on campus? No wonder she'd gone out on only five dates in the four years she'd lived in Kansas City for her degree.

She pulled off her hoodie and sat cross-legged against the tufted headboard. Her cabin was immense and luxurious like everything else on the ship. The king bed was a guilty pleasure, too large for a single girl who wouldn't be sharing it with anyone else. She'd stretched in all directions the night before, not even coming close to the edge. Even the bathroom was built for a couple, with double shower heads, double vanities, double fluffy, ultra-white towels. Was she supposed to use both sets of towels or only one?

Outside the wide French doors, on a narrow balcony, two chairs flanked a small table. Maybe later, when the sun shone to the west, she'd sit outside and gaze at the city of Porto, putting her feet up on the second chair.

The memory of her bedroom in her tiny apartment back home sprang to mind, so much smaller than this cabin and certainly lacking all the amenities this one boasted. Everything she'd left in Kansas was clouded in uncertainty—a foreign feeling after living there all her life—and she still had a hard time reconciling the only reality she'd ever known with her new privileged circumstances.

But who wouldn't? She'd gone to bed one night counting her pennies for the rest of the month, and she'd woken up to find out she was a Portuguese heiress. If there was an easy way to adjust to that, no one had told her. The position didn't come with a manual. Furthermore, Dad hadn't wanted her to come and Grandfather now wanted her to stay. And she didn't know what she wanted.

Vanessa suppressed a laugh. Just a few weeks ago she'd been watching the sun set over the Kansas plains, as she'd done as long as she could remember. But that was a whole world away and harder and harder to remember with each day spent in Portugal.

All thanks to Grandfather who was responsible for the drastic change in her life. He actually saw himself as the hero who'd rescued her from her pitiful existence in Kansas. Yet, she couldn't bring herself to commend him for it or for anything else, not after all the anxiety and confusion he'd caused for the past weeks.

Like this trip he'd sent her on and the captain he'd asked to spy on her.

There she was, thinking of the captain again. Vanessa pulled out her phone. It was too early for breakfast, and she didn't want to call down to the kitchen, even if the crew thought of her as a VIP passenger. Such a strange situation to be in.

Vanessa pulled up the search engine on her smart-phone and typed *Captain Romano* and *Princess Catarina*. The links and pictures came up immediately. She followed a link to Gold River Cruises, Grandfather's company, where Captain Matias Romano had been working for the past sixteen years, according to the information she read. Another page pointed to a small entry about the captain himself: Ernesto Matias da Silva Romano, age thirty-one, born in Porto, Portugal. His parents were briefly mentioned, but there was nothing about a wife or children. He didn't wear a wedding ring, but that was hardly a reliable indication of his present marital status.

On the company's website, a picture of the *Princess Catarina* at the christening ceremony three years ago showed Captain Romano next to a striking woman who had long black hair and wore a red cocktail dress. Maybe he did have a wife after all and she was very selective about her public appearances.

Vanessa blew out a breath and put the phone to sleep. It didn't matter if the captain was married. That had nothing to do with his job and certainly less to do with her. Didn't Dad always say that too much interest was almost as bad as too little expectation? Vanessa had learned the hard way, expecting as much of others as she did of herself. The disappointment was hard to take at times. She hadn't learned to curb her curiosity either.

The phone rattled against the surface of the bed-side table. Vanessa swiped at the screen and groaned when Dad's number showed up. She hesitated for a second before accepting the call.

"Vanessa. About time," Dad said by way of greeting.

She sat on the bed. "Hi, Dad, how are you?"

"I've been calling you and leaving messages, and you didn't answer."

Even after she'd left for college, Dad had a hard time letting go of checking on her. "I'm answering now, Dad. I was busy last night at the captain's dinner."

"A fancy dinner, I bet." He paused for a deep breath. "What's the ship like?"

"It's very nice." Vanessa held back a sigh of her own, leaned against the headboard, and settled in for a longer conversation than she wanted. "You'd like it, Dad. The woodwork is impressive." She spent the next ten minutes answering his reluctant questions. He was curious, but didn't want to show it. Vanessa described the details she knew he'd be interested in, but not so much as to make it obvious. Her being away on this trip and aboard the ship was already hard enough on him.

She closed her eyes after hanging up. Usually, he called her only every few days, but his calls had become more frequent since she'd arrived in Portugal. Which was unfortunate because Dad's earnestness could only be taken in small doses.

After a quick shower, she changed into her favorite pair of dark skinny jeans and added a thin cardigan over a gauzy top and chunky necklace. She pulled her hair into a low ponytail and applied some light make-up. It was only breakfast, and dressy casual was probably fine.

In truth, the dress code caused her some anxiety. Before the trip, Vanessa had read blogs on river cruises and social procedures aboard five-star ships. Despite her reluctance, being prepared made more sense. Her lack of knowledge would probably appall some of her fellow passengers but, at this point, Vanessa could only hope they wouldn't see right through her inexperience.

What about the captain? Did he know this was her first time on a cruise? How much had Grandfather told him?

She glanced at the full-size mirror behind the door one last time. Much better than this morning when she'd seen the captain near the bridge. The key-card went in the front pocket of her jeans.

She was ready to face the day. . . and Captain Romano.

CHAPTER THREE

*E*arly breakfast was served in the lounge on the upper deck. At first impression, the room didn't differ too much from the restaurant: same layout, same row of panoramic windows flanked by curtains. The fewer tables were arranged closer to the bar, a gleaming curve of brass and polished wood and the focal point of the meticulously decorated room. Seating areas of leather sofas and comfortable chairs, interspersed with side tables and lamps, filled the center of the room, and, at the far end, the hardwood dance floor awaited the evening entertainment.

But the space was mostly empty of passengers, a strong contrast to the night before at dinner.

Vanessa had expected a buffet-style breakfast, but there were no sideboards laden with food. Instead, the tables were set with breakfast plates, and a few servers carried jugs of orange juice and water.

From a round table, an arm shot up and waved at her. It belonged to one of the English ladies, who sat with two other passengers. What was her name?

"Miss Clark, how surprising to see you out and about so early in the morning," the lady said when Vanessa approached the table. "I'm Mrs. Grantham. We met last night at dinner."

Grantham, that was her name. "Yes, I remember. How are you doing, Mrs. Grantham? Please, call me Vanessa."

"You must call me Agnes. We don't stand on ceremony around here. Don't let the fancy ship intimidate you." She gestured to the other ladies. "These are my friends, Priscilla Smith and Ruth Camden. Please, sit with us."

Vanessa pulled out a chair across from Agnes Grantham. "Thank you. I'll stay until your husbands arrive." She certainly didn't want to impose on anyone.

The group chuckled. "They won't be coming up for a while," Ruth Camden offered with a wide smile. "They're old and rickety and enjoy their beds too much." The others agreed with a round of winks and nods.

A server approached and filled Vanessa's cup with coffee. Another server set a plate with warm rolls, European-style croissants, and a bowl of fresh-cut fruit in front of her. At the center of the table, several platters with butter, jams, Portuguese pastries, and an array of sliced cheeses and deli meats rounded up the breakfast menu.

Vanessa thanked the servers. Her stomach rumbled, and she reached for a fresh croissant.

"How did you spend your first night aboard, Vanessa?" Agnes asked her.

"Very comfortably." It wasn't the bed's fault she'd spent half the night thinking about the captain.

Ruth signaled the closest server and asked for another pot of tea. She then turned to Vanessa. "Is this your first holiday in Portugal?"

Her friend added, "What do you think of the ship so far?"

Vanessa swallowed a bite of fluffy crust and savory butter. Was it that obvious? She turned to Ruth. "Yes, it's my first time in Portugal." Then she addressed Priscilla. "It's a very impressive ship, and I'm looking forward to the trip up the river. I've read it's a beautiful itinerary." What else could she say? That her grandfather had practically forced her to come?

"Oh, it is. We come back every year and love it," said Agnes. The other ladies nodded in agreement.

Vanessa looked up from her plate. "You've done this trip before?"

"Oh yes. We've been taking this trip for a few years," said Priscilla.

Agnes nodded. "It's a tradition."

"In England we're too busy with grandchildren, Friends of the Library, the Botanical Society, and myriad other things." Agnes gestured at her friends and their respective activities. "So we take this trip once a year to spend time with one another." She smiled and her friends nodded and smiled in return.

"Every year?" Vanessa asked.

"Well, there was one year we took a cruise of the French Riviera, but it wasn't quite the same." Ruth shook her head.

"Don't get us wrong," Agnes rushed to add. "It was very nice, but it didn't quite suit us. So we returned to Gold River Cruises the following year."

"Captain Romano is the best," Priscilla said.

Vanessa looked between the three of the them. "You mean you take this very trip every year with the same ship and captain?"

"Oh yes. It wouldn't be the same without Captain Romano and his crew, now would it?" Agnes took a sip of tea, her eyes softening into a contented expression.

Vanessa didn't have a reply. She'd met the captain only yesterday and already he occupied more space in her thoughts than she ought to give him. Not that he knew about it, and she intended to keep it that way.

"And you, dear? How did you discover this cruise?" The curious look on Agnes's face mirrored that of her friends.

"It was a gift." Vanessa set her glass down. "From my grandfather."

"Has he taken the trip before, then?" Priscilla asked.

"Yes, I think so." Did the river cruise company's president take the trip? She didn't know Grandfather well enough to understand how he ran his company or his life.

The ladies squared their shoulders and looked up at someone behind Vanessa.

"Good morning, ladies."

The deep, familiar voice sounded over her right shoulder, and Vanessa turned to see Captain Romano standing by the neighboring chair. He greeted each lady by her surname and spent a few moments asking pertinent questions about each one. The English ladies smiled and cooed at him, and Vanessa suppressed a smile at the interchange.

He turned to her then and nodded. "Good morning, Miss Clark."

That voice. It resonated inside her. Vanessa sat straight in her chair and resisted the urge to smooth the flyaway hairs against her neck. She'd seen the captain just a few hours before and yet her heart beat a little faster at the sight of him, and at the sound of his smooth voice. Foolish, foolish heart.

She held his gaze and greeted him back. "Good morning, Captain Romano." She couldn't roll the *R*s like the English ladies did. They must have practiced.

From across the table, she felt the eyes of her fellow passengers as they witnessed the exchange between her and the captain. The small group sat in silence and obvious adoration of the man. He most assuredly had a group of fans and he didn't seem to mind the attention.

"You're too kind, Captain Romano, to take the time to greet us," said Agnes. "We know how busy you are this morning."

He pulled his attention away from Vanessa and looked at Agnes Grantham. "True, we are busy, but not so much that I can't say hello to my favorite group of passengers." The ladies tittered, and he gave them a half smile.

His eyes touched Vanessa's. More of a flick than a true look, and she'd have missed it if she hadn't been looking at him. Did he mean to include her in the remark about his favorites?

"Besides, we have all the procedures down to a routine," he added. "We'll be leaving soon after lunch and on schedule."

So much for being on schedule. Matias hurried down the service staircase to the lower deck and quickly walked the length of the straight hall leading to the galley. When he arrived, the head chef and the cruise director stood in front of each other talking at the same time in very unfriendly terms.

He held his hands up and they stopped. "Ladies, what's going on?"

They both knew better than to need his help sorting anything out. Miguel could roll the ship out of the dock just as well as Matias could, but the passengers expected the captain to be at the helm, and Matias always did what the passengers wanted.

Within reason.

Chef Teresa threw her hands in the air. "We

had a problem with the refrigerators over-night."
Matias rose an eyebrow at her and she hurried on.
"Everything's under control, Captain. You know I can
handle emergencies."

Matias nodded at the chef. She was old enough to
be his grandmother—she even shared the same name
as his own grandmother— and there was pretty much
nothing that intimidated her. She'd been on the crew
of his former ship and since the maiden voyage of
the *Princess Catarina,* and her years of experience
as an acclaimed regional chef attracted passengers
just as much as the itinerary. Besides, Matias liked
her no-nonsense attitude.

"What I can't handle is people interfering in my
kitchen when they don't—"

Miss Rialto interrupted. "I'm only doing my job,
Captain. If there will be changes to the menu, I need
to know what those are beforehand." She was the
youngest cruise director he'd worked with, and this
was her third trip on his crew. So far, he liked her
sense of rapport with the passengers, but he had
not worked with her long enough to know how she
reacted under more stressful conditions.

"Chef Teresa. Miss Rialto." Matias looked at each
woman in turn. "We all know that both of you are
capable professionals. I don't see a reason why you
can't work this problem out between the two of you."

"Yes, Captain." They nodded at him and glanced
askance at each other. He turned around and left.
They'd keep busy this morning. Chef Teresa had

lunch and dinner to worry about, and Miss Rialto was taking the passengers on a city excursion around Porto after breakfast.

Despite the three-deck climb, he avoided the elevator and took the stairs quickly. Breakfast was now in full swing in the dining room, and he greeted the passengers he passed in the reception area on their way to be seated. His eyes lingered for a moment, searching for a certain face but she wasn't there. Matias placed his attention back on getting to the bridge on time.

Miguel and the other two junior officers waited for him to go over the schedule. Pedro and Jaime took turns relieving Matias and Miguel in the bridge as necessary, and since they had other duties as well, it was crucial to coordinate their shifts and go over the on-board protocols.

The internal phone rang and he took it. "This is Captain Romano in the bridge."

"This is Chef Teresa in the kitchen." Her voice came over fast and flustered. "Captain, I need you to authorize the coming of a repairman aboard."

Matias gripped the phone tighter. "I thought you said you had everything under control."

"I thought I did, sir, but the main refrigerator needs a new thermostat before I lose all the prep for today and tomorrow morning." She took a breath. "I already found a guy who has the part, and he can be here in half an hour. I just need you to authorize his coming aboard."

"Yes, I'll call the receptionist."

"Thank you, Captain." The relief in her voice was obvious.

"Chef Teresa, will this part take care of the problem for the rest of the trip?"

"Yes, Captain, it will." She sounded weary, and Matias made a mental note to go see her in the kitchen after the lunch rush.

He called reception and let them know a repairman was coming aboard soon.

After the meeting on the bridge, Matias stood on the port side of the sun deck and watched the passengers as they went ashore for the excursion. Three charter buses waited up the street from the dock to take everyone on the two-hour tour through the city.

Miss Clark was among them. The last of the early-morning fog had finally burned off, and she was dressed for the warmer weather. A wide-brimmed hat adorned her head, her hair caught at the nape of her neck. She wore over-sized sunglasses, white, cropped pants, and a navy top with white stripes—a definite nod to the nautical theme. Most likely, the outfit was purposeful. She didn't seem to be the kind of girl who left things to chance. She was too assertive for that.

She stood to the side of the group, and when Miss Rialto gestured at the ship, Miss Clark turned to look as the others did. Matias waved at them, and they returned the gesture, nodding at Miss Rialto's words of caution. He knew the script, and this was the part where she warned the passengers about keeping close to the group and making it back on time.

Before circling the closest bus, Miss Clark raised her fingers and touched the brim of her hat in his direction, and he could imagine her lips pulled in a teasing smile even if he couldn't see them.

Matias shook his head and chuckled. Sassy was the word that came to mind. She was sassy and well aware of it. Most likely proud as well.

This would be an interesting trip.

CHAPTER FOUR

$\mathcal{M}$atias exited his cabin and closed the door behind him. It was lunch time. The passengers had returned from the excursion a half hour ago and should have now been in the dining room for the lunch buffet. Precisely an hour later, Matias would pull the ship from the dock and commence the cruise up the river Douro.

This was the exciting part for him—something he never tired of. He loved to see the expressions on the passengers' faces as they watched the landscape change with the ship's progression, the steady pressure of the prow on the water as it gently cut a path between the depth buoys on both sides of the river.

"Captain Romano." Miss Rialto called him as he reached the stairs to the main deck.

He nodded at her. "Yes, I know. I'm on my way to the dining room."

He moved toward the first step, but she blocked his path. "May I have a word with you, Captain?"

Matias arched an eyebrow. "Right now? Is this a pressing matter, or can it wait?"

"I'm afraid it's urgent, Captain."

Matias walked around the staircase where they'd be out of prying eyes but still in a public area. "Well?" he urged.

Miss Rialto took a breath. "I can't seem to locate Miss Clark, the young American."

"Yes, I know who Miss Clark is. What do you mean, you can't locate her? Didn't she go ashore with the excursion?"

"Yes, she did." Miss Rialto looked away at the staircase and then back at the carpeted floor.

"And didn't she return with everybody else? She should be in the dining room having lunch with the rest of the passengers."

She shifted her weight. "She got on bus number three but I can't remember seeing her return aboard the *Princess Catarina*."

A sense of dread froze the pit of Matias's stomach. "What do you mean, you don't remember her boarding?"

"I'm afraid I was distracted with Mr. and Mrs. Smith and can't remember if Miss Clark came aboard when we arrived."

The back of his neck broke in a cold sweat, and the air conditioning vent directly above him blew his skin into gooseflesh. "Did you check in the dining room?" He turned to the staircase. "Tell me on the way there."

Miss Rialto nodded. "She's not in the dining room or in the lounge."

"What about her cabin?"

Had Miss Clark left the ship as she'd hinted at the day before? Matias had seen her at early breakfast, and she hadn't said anything about leaving.

When he and Miss Rialto reached the upper deck, Matias asked for a master key card from the receptionist. They walked to Miss Clark's cabin and knocked on the door.

At the lack of response, he handed the key card to Miss Rialto. "Open the door and go in, please." She hesitated, and he pushed it into her hand. "Call out if you find anything."

Miss Rialto entered the cabin and called out for Miss Clark, but no one replied. Matias stood at the open doorway and rubbed at the back of his neck.

Miss Clark was an adult and free to leave if she'd wanted, but what would he tell her grandfather?

After a few minutes, Miss Rialto appeared back at the door and opened it wide. "She's not here."

"What about her belongings?"

"Everything appears to be in order. The suitcase is at the bottom of the closet and her clothes are hanging inside. She also has toiletries in the bathroom."

So Miss Clark hadn't planned to leave the ship, unless she'd purposefully left her things behind, which was unlikely.

"Miss Rialto, go to the dining room and carry on as usual. I'll take over this."

She hesitated for a moment but then nodded and took the stairs down to the main deck.

Matias called for Jaime and Pedro and within minutes the three of them started a search of all the common areas on the ship, moving to the crew-only areas afterward. They didn't find her. He sent them back to their duties and returned to the bridge.

"Nothing?" Miguel asked when Matias entered the small space which also served as the captain's office.

Matias shook his head. "Unless she's hiding in someone else's cabin, which she has no reason to do."

Miguel looked at the round clock on the wall behind them. "Lunch will be over soon."

"Well, I can't delay the departure on account of one passenger." Even if the passenger was the company president's granddaughter.

Some of the passengers who had finished lunch had trickled up to the sun deck, and they sat on the lounge chairs under the awning and in the sun. Matias hurried down to the dining room. He ate there for most meals, but he was short on time since he'd been searching for Miss Clark, and planned to get a plate to go and eat it at the bridge.

The room was still half-full, with several people lingering in conversation over their desserts and espressos. Miss Rialto sat at a table with a couple he hadn't met yet, maps and brochures amid the dessert plates and coffee cups. Most likely, they were first timers and had questions about the itinerary and daily excursions. Some passengers always required a little more hand-holding than others did, and it was the job of the cruise director and the excursion guides to provide whatever support they asked for.

As Matias turned to exit the dining room, Miss Clark walked in through the doors. They stopped a few paces away from each other.

She offered a half smile and pointed at his plate. "Am I too late for lunch?"

He looked at her for a long moment, a firm grip on the covered plate of food in his hand. She'd changed into a long, flowy skirt and a tank top, her hair held back by a headband. Her freckled shoulders stood out in contrast to the light fabric lending her skin a healthy glow.

A million questions ran through his mind, but this was not the place or time for it. "No, Miss Clark, you're not too late for lunch."

She smiled. "Good. I'm hungry." She took a step toward the buffet.

"Miss Clark, will you please meet me at the bridge in one hour?" He had to find out why she'd left the group.

She halted, her forehead wrinkled in little folds between her eyebrows. Even in a confused state, she was still attractive.

Matias stopped himself and the direction of his thoughts. If anything, he was irritated at her and he wanted to know where she'd been for the past few

hours. He didn't need to notice her charming quali-
ties, physical or otherwise.

Not waiting for her reply, he left for the upper
deck.

Once there, he shed his jacket and hung it on
the hanger behind the door. He ate quickly then he
and Miguel ran the departure checklist, and within
minutes the *Princess Catarina* pulled away from the
dock and commenced her ascent up the River Douro.
Only ten minutes behind schedule. Matias let out
a slow breath.

Miss Rialto' voice came over the PA system as she
recited the script about the history of the city of Porto
and the River Douro, giving particular attention to
the six bridges as they passed under them. He knew
all the words by heart and could recite them just as
well as she did.

A few of the passengers emerged from below—the
more adventurous or agile ones. The upper, main,
and lower decks were serviced by an elevator and
a wide staircase, but only a ladder was available to
reach the sun deck. The passengers stood near the
railings, mostly to the port side, and some walked by
the bridge, but the prow was cordoned off.

Matias maneuvered the familiar waterway, a sense
of calm and assurance filling his chest. His heartbeat
slowed, and his breathing evened out at the feel of
the brass wheel on the skin of his palms, warm and
solid and comforting. It was here, on the water and
behind the wheel, that he most felt at home, where

he found his center and his purpose. Here, the river commanded everything, and Matias was as one with the ship in bringing the passengers safely through the verdant waters.

After a while, Miguel took over at the wheel. Matias retrieved the itinerary and skimmed it, confirming what he already knew about the daily schedule. The passenger list was attached, a grid of names by cabin number in neat, even rows.

Something was off. He stopped and read the list again. "It's not even," he said.

"What's not even?" Miguel looked over his shoulder.

Matias tapped the paper with his pen. "The number of passengers is not even."

The numbers were always the same: one eighty-meter long ship with 2 engines; 65 cabins, 130 passengers, and 40 crew members. Same numbers, same routine.

But not this time.

"That's right." Miguel kept his eyes straight ahead. "Cabin two has only one passenger, instead of the usual couple."

Miss Clark was the single occupant in cabin number two, and, as a result, there were only 129 passengers aboard on this trip. Matias dropped the papers on the surface of the wooden counter and stood, rubbing the back of his neck. How had he missed that?

Miguel shook his head. "You're not hung up on that silly numbers thing again, are you?"

Matias gathered the papers and placed them back where they belonged inside the folder. "Maybe. Maybe not."

Miguel teased him about it, and other crew members talked behind his back. To them, it was a childish superstition. To him, it was a portent of bad luck.

And that was the last thing he needed on this trip.

Vanessa took her time arriving at the sun deck. She'd been the last one at lunch and the captain hadn't seemed too happy to find her there. Why did he want to see her at the bridge anyway? She was not looking forward to this meeting.

She'd left her sun hat behind in her cabin and didn't want to go back for it. After the early fog and colder temperatures this morning, the weather had turned out warm and sunny and perfect for a late summer day. The captain had pulled the ship away from the dock fifteen minutes before, and Vanessa had watched the city go by from the observation balcony just off the lounge on the upper deck. Other passengers had the same idea, and the small space quickly became crowded. Once on the sun deck, she found a place in the shade by the railing alongside a few passengers who were already there.

The view was better from the sun deck, and the differences surprised her. The contrast between Porto by night and Porto by day, Porto from downtown and Porto from a moving ship. In the past few weeks since her arrival, she'd grown to appreciate the city. Grandfather would be thrilled to know her opinion had changed some, but Vanessa didn't have any plans to tell him. Let him think she still hated everything about Porto. He didn't deserve more.

She'd never traveled so far before. A few trips to Texas during high school didn't count; not compared to Europe, where everything was so different and there was so much to learn every day. How could this all be part of her heritage when she'd grown up without any knowledge of it? She didn't feel half-Portuguese.

The crushing sense of being overwhelmed had abated some, but it was still hard to understand the scope of what it all meant for her future. Dad hadn't said much other than confirming that she indeed had a Portuguese grandfather with a fortune. Dad owed her a lot of explanations when she returned from this trip.

Soon the urban landscape of tightly packed buildings and old façades gave way to a more rural view of rolling hills and scarce village houses interspersed with pines and eucalyptus trees. The world-famous wine country of tiered parcels with neatly arranged grapevines was still up ahead on the trip.

One of the young deckhands approached her. Vanessa had seen him work with the captain before and knew he must be one of his assistants.

"Miss Clark, Captain Romano will see you now. This way, please." He gestured toward the bridge.

Several passengers paused to watch them. Vanessa didn't pay any attention to them and followed the deckhand.

When she arrived at the bridge, the Captain stood by a tall desk. Another crewman maneuvered the helm, the one she'd seen the day before. He looked at her with a friendly expression and nodded in acknowledgment.

"Thanks for coming, Miss Clark. This is my second-in-command, Miguel Freitas."

Vanessa smiled and nodded back.

Why had the captain asked her to come? She waited for him to say something more. Her nerves rose with each passing minute, and the awkward pause only added to her sense of discomfort. After Captain Romano checked the wall clock for a second time, Vanessa gathered her courage to ask him.

The phone rang and she jumped.

Captain Romano turned away from her and answered it. "Yes, sir," he said. He repeated the same line three more times before turning in her direction. He pushed a button and set the receiver down on the desk surface. "You're now on speaker, sir."

"Vanessa, this is your grandfather speaking."

Her eyes widened and she gasped. "Grandfather?"

"I had hoped it didn't have to come to this, but after your little display this morning, you leave me no choice." His voice sounded firm yet a bit weary, as if he scolded a disobedient child.

Vanessa recovered from her shock. "I have no idea what you're talking about."

The captain had the decency of looking guilty and uncomfortable while his crewman pretended not to notice anything else than the wheel of the ship and the expanse of river ahead.

Grandfather spoke again. "I know you probably don't understand, but your safety is of the utmost importance to me." He paused, and Vanessa shook her head, disbelieving the situation. What did Grandfather want and why did he have to do it in front of the captain?

He went on. "I've made lots of enemies in my career and some of them would like nothing better than to know I have brought on a grandchild to take over in a few years."

No, she hadn't agreed to that yet. "Grandfather—"

He interrupted her. "Vanessa, please listen. I only have a few minutes before my next appointment. I've had a security detail on you since you arrived in the country. I thought with you being on this cruise, I could relax a little. In fact, you were the one who insisted you didn't need a bodyguard while on the ship."

Vanessa shook her head and looked at the captain.

"At the next port, I'll have the security detail join the cruise to keep an eye on you," Grandfather said.

"For heaven's sake, what are you talking about?" Vanessa raised her voice, unable to hold back the frustration from her tone.

Captain Romano rubbed his neck behind his ear. "Sir, wait a minute there—"

Grandfather let out a long breath. "Vanessa, where were you this morning? You went ashore with the excursion group but you didn't return with them. Captain Romano doesn't think I know, but I do."

The captain stilled and raised his head to look at the phone and then at Vanessa.

"Well, where were you?" Grandfather asked.

This couldn't be happening. He was treating her like a child, and he believed he had the right to do it.

"I— I left the group to visit a part of town I hadn't seen yet and then I took a cab back to the dock."

"Vanessa, that's the kind of thing you can't do," Grandfather said. "That's why I wanted a security detail with you at all times."

Vanessa's shoulders slumped. Would he listen to her if she asked him not to send anyone to follow her around?

For a moment, only silence filled the small room. Vanessa folded her arms and took a deep breath, Grandfather's words running through her mind. He'd had a security detail following her for her protection since the first day, he'd said, not just for the trip as he'd suggested. As if she were an investment. Was this how the rich and powerful lived their lives?

Grandfather cleared his throat. "Captain Romano, my granddaughter's safety is at stake here. I know she doesn't want a bodyguard. Given the circumstances, I'm going to ask you to accompany her when she goes ashore. I think that's the best solution for the time being."

Vanessa slid to a bar-height chair and faced the captain who'd walked closer to the phone. His forehead wrinkled and he scrubbed a spot on his temple. "Yes, sir," he said.

He clearly did not want the job.

"Excuse me, what did you say?" Grandfather asked, his voice laced with impatience. "Speak louder, Captain," he barked.

"I said I will watch your granddaughter, sir." Captain Romano enunciated his words, the resolution unequivocal. His shoulders set straight and his jaw squared as if he'd just offered up his life in sacrifice to protect a royal princess. But she wasn't a princess; just a girl from Kansas. And she had to put a stop to this nonsense.

"Wait a minute." Vanessa jumped from her chair and stood next to the captain. "I don't need—"

"Vanessa, it's not a question of what you don't need," Grandfather interrupted. "Captain Romano, are you serious with your acceptance? Do you know what it fully means?"

"I'll accompany her when she goes ashore, and I'll keep an eye on her while on the ship," Captain Romano said. "And if you're worried about my availability, I can delegate some of my other duties." He glanced at the other guy, who raised a thumbs-up, still piloting the ship and still looking ahead.

"Grandfather, this is not—."

"Please, Vanessa," Grandfather interrupted again. "Let me and Captain Romano take care of everything."

The dread that had been building in her since she'd passed through the door soured her stomach, and she touched the spot. It was useless. They didn't care what she thought. Neither one of them did.

While the captain and Grandfather discussed the particulars of their arrangement, Vanessa slipped out of the bridge.

CHAPTER FIVE

*T*he next morning, Vanessa climbed the stairs to the sun deck. The first rays hadn't peeked yet but the sky was clear and the air smelled a little brisk. She stood to the right, facing the river and the bank on the other side. Behind her, to the left of the ship, the small town of Entre-Os-Rios still lay dormant and somewhat mysterious in the early morning. A church bell counted the hours in snappy, short clangs and a dog not too far away howled in reply.

Dinner had been awkward between her and Captain Romano the night before, but fortunately sitting with six other people had effectively prevented any chance for a private conversation. Afterward, Vanessa had sought the company of the English ladies and had sat with them in the lounge. Twice the captain had approached the group to greet them and twice Vanessa had avoided eye contact with him.

He'd wanted to talk to her; she knew that. But her feelings about the phone call from Grandfather still burned too hot, and she needed space and time to let them simmer down and wane. In the end, she'd slept even worse than the previous night, and here she was on deck earlier than the second morning, hoping Captain Romano would initiate contact. How long could she hold on to her pride and stubbornness and expect everything to resolve itself?

The ship had docked at their first stop yesterday evening after a leisurely pace through the first leg of the trip. They'd passed the first three dams in the afternoon, and Vanessa had watched from the balcony at the prow of the upper deck. She'd spent some time reading on the balcony in her cabin and being distracted by the view on the port side of the ship. The landscape was different, so different from what she knew. As trite as it sounded, the same thought came to her. Everywhere she looked, the novelty of sights and sounds and textures called out to her, even from her spot on the ship.

Vanessa chanced a look at the bridge. The captain and his firstmate stood hunched over the desk and talked animatedly. As if sensing her, Captain Romano raised his head and locked his eyes on her. Vanessa turned back to the view and took her phone out of her pocket to keep her hands busy. Her cheeks heated, and she swallowed down a curse. Why wasn't she over the silly blushing by now? It wasn't reasonable to feel this way over a guy she'd just barely met and who probably didn't even like her. She gave herself a mental shake.

Her phone vibrated in her hands, and a text from Dad popped up on the screen.

How are things going, Vanessa?

Was it wrong to hope Dad hadn't heard about the previous day's fiasco? He and Grandfather weren't on the best of terms so Vanessa counted on that. She typed a quick reply.

Everything's great.

No sense in telling him. Dad would only overreact like Grandfather and the captain had, then worry that he was far away and couldn't do anything to help.

Anything fun on the schedule today? Dad asked.

Going ashore later. It was supposed to be fun, but having the captain with her would probably ruin that.

Have a good day.

She replied with a smile emoji.

The door to the bridge creaked open. Vanessa returned her phone to her front pocket and resisted the urge to turn around.

"Vanessa," the captain called in a low voice.

He needn't worry about anyone overhearing them since there was no one else around.

She took a quick breath. He was using her name. Her first name.

"Miss Clark," he said louder and with more insistence.

This time, Vanessa turned to him, and he gestured for her to come inside the bridge. His hair, perfectly styled every other time she'd seen him, appeared slightly mussed, as if he might have run a hand through it in frustration. And the knot of his tie hung a bit off center, maybe from being tugged a few times.

"What's going on?" she asked after he closed the door behind her.

He exchanged a glance with the other guy, who sat in front of a console with a keyboard and computer-like screen. "Just an inconvenience. Hopefully we'll figure it out soon."

Vanessa peeked at the console. "What kind of inconvenience?"

Captain Romano handed Vanessa a cup. "I was hoping you'd come out on the prow this morning." He paused while she took the cup in her hands. "I think we need to talk about your grandfather's phone call yesterday."

"I know you want to talk, but I'd rather not." She took a sip and was surprised by the bold flavor. "Hot chocolate?"

The captain's voice softened. "Do you like it? It's a special blend of dark chocolate with a shot of espresso." He held up a plate with croissants. "I had planned a better breakfast on the prow, but with this"—he gestured toward the console—"uh, problem, I'm afraid I'm not as available as I thought I'd be."

Was that an apology? His expression didn't give her any clues to how he felt and she could only make assumptions about the meaning behind his words. But, in her experience, assumptions rarely yielded good results.

Vanessa put down the cup and croissant and stepped closer to the console. "What kind of problem is it?"

Captain Romano passed a hand through his hair, which he'd apparently already been doing. "It's okay. Don't worry about it."

Vanessa approached the captain's crewman. "Can you remind me of your name, please?"

"Just call me Miguel." His mouth turned up in a small smile, and his brown eyes twinkled in a boyish expression.

"No rank or title?" She asked.

"I'm not the captain; he is." He tipped his chin in the captain's direction.

She smiled back. "Okay, Miguel. What's going on with the computer?"

Captain Romano cleared his throat. "Miss Clark, we'll take care of it. We called the IT guy at the main office, but he's checking something more pressing at the lower deck."

She glanced from the console to him. "Will you let me take a look?"

His forehead wrinkled. "Are you a computer expert?"

"You could say that." Vanessa waved a hand. "Why don't you tell me what's going on? I'll be able to see if I can help in five minutes or less, and it won't cost you anything."

Captain Romano hesitated. "It's not normal to ask passengers for help with the computer system."

"And what has been normal about this trip so far?" Miguel said in a tone that left no doubts to how he felt about the situation. What was not normal?

The captain looked at him, and Vanessa followed the silent exchange. Captain Romano was swayed but didn't want to admit it so quickly. Was it because of her or because of the rules?

At last, he gestured toward the chair. "We don't know what to make of it. Every time we type anything, it comes out all gibberish."

Vanessa sat down, and Miguel scooted back, allowing her more room at the console.

"Has this happened before?" She poised herself at the keyboard and typed a sentence.

"No, this was the first time," replied Miguel. Captain Romano nodded.

She typed again and turned to them. "I know what the problem is and it's an easy fix."

They both visibly relaxed. "What is it?" The captain asked.

"Something very simple." Vanessa typed a few more times as she restored the right settings. "But it's obvious that someone played a prank on you." She stood and turned the keyboard in Captain Romano's direction.

He sat down and typed a few words. "How did you fix it so quickly? We've been at it for a couple of hours and couldn't figure it out."

Miguel leaned over the console verifying that it indeed worked well. "And what do you mean about a prank?"

Vanessa pulled up another chair closer to the console and helped herself to a croissant. "Someone changed the settings on your keyboard. It's called an alternative keyboard layout. In this case the Dvorak keyboard."

They both looked at her with blank expressions and wrinkled brows.

Vanessa gestured toward the keyboard. "This keyboard on your console is a QWERTY, like most keyboards everywhere. A Dvorak keyboard has the keys used most often within closer reach of your fingers, supposedly to increase productivity and typing speed. When someone changes a QWERTY to a Dvorak, they also need to change the keys so the typing matches what you see on the screen." She leaned back and took a sip of her drink. "From your reaction, I'm guessing you didn't know any of this."

Captain Romano stood from the console. "So you're saying this was not an accident?"

She shook her head. "Whoever did this knew what they were doing."

Another charged look passed between him and his firstmate.

Vanessa's curiosity took over. "Who has access to this room?"

"Miguel and I are the only ones who have keys. Key cards, actually. Security is monitored remotely, and they record every time the door is locked and unlocked."

"Which means you'd know if someone else has been in here." Vanessa looked at the corners of the ceiling. Did they also have camera monitors?

Captain Romano followed her gaze. "And yes, we have security cameras as well."

"Is it okay for me to be here?" Was someone looking at the live footage from the bridge of the *Princess Catarina* wondering who she was and what she was doing there?

The captain waved a hand and his expression relaxed. "Of course you're fine. I invited you here."

He didn't say *duh,* but it was definitely implied. Vanessa nodded.

"What about those two young guys who follow you around?"

"Jaime and Pedro. They're our assistants and junior officers. They also have other duties, but they take our place when one of us is not in here." He gestured between himself and Miguel.

"Could someone have made this switch remotely?" Miguel asked.

"Absolutely," Vanessa said. He meant hacking, even if he hadn't used the word. "And it wouldn't be too difficult either," she added, anticipating his next question.

She stood and tucked the chair back in its place against the far end on the counter. "I'll leave so you can return to work now that your keyboard is back in business."

Miguel was already engrossed in whatever task required his attention.

Captain Romano opened the door and accompanied Vanessa onto the sun deck. "I can't thank you enough for the help, Vanessa. I mean, Miss Clark." He walked beside her as they moved on to the railing facing the river.

"You can call me Vanessa, Captain," she said in a light tone. "And I was glad to help. Hope you catch the hacker who did this."

For a moment, he looked at her with a puzzled expression. He turned to watch a small barge go by in the river and waved at the two men inside who held their arms up in greeting. The silence between her and the Captain stretched for a few minutes. Maybe she'd said something wrong and he didn't want to comment on it.

He broke the silence. "I'll call you Vanessa if you'll call me Matias."

Her heart jumped. An idiotic smile made a move to her lips, but she quickly put a stop to that. It was a reasonable request from him; nothing more. She had just called his firstmate by his first name, after all. It wouldn't do anything to go reading more into his words.

"Even in front of the other passengers?" Everyone addressed him as Captain.

He seemed to consider it for a moment. "Well, maybe when there's no one else around."

As he looked straight ahead, the corners of his mouth rose in a lazy smile.

Matias bent over the schedule and the itinerary one last time. There were two excursions today, one in the morning and one in the afternoon. With some adjustments and flexibility, he could accompany Vanessa ashore and make it back for departure.

If everything went well.

Miguel stood at the wheel, his feet planted apart and his hands firmly gripped. "Are you still looking at that schedule?" He glanced back at him. "You know I don't mind taking the ship to the next port, if it comes to that."

Matias nodded in reply. Most likely, it would come to that. After years and years of straightforward trips with nothing to report, karma had caught up with him. Only the third day, and already he'd had to write a page worth of reporting for each day of this trip. It wasn't much consolation to be right when it involved extra work and added worry.

"Don't over-think it, Captain." Miguel said. "Just go ashore with her and have some fun."

Matias straightened and stepped away from the counter. "That's the problem."

"Leaving the ship?" Miguel asked.

"Having too much fun."

Miguel raised an eyebrow at him. "When was the last time you went ashore with a woman?"

Matias didn't have to reply. Miguel knew the answer just as well as he did.

As Pedro walked in the door to keep Miguel company in the bridge, Matias put the phone in his pocket. "Don't have too much fun without me," he said to Miguel.

Miguel chuckled. "Yes, sir, Captain Romano."

Miss Clark was not on the sun deck in her usual spot. He found her by the swimming pool on a chaise lounge, her enormous hat blocking her face, and a pair of oversize sunglasses perched on her nose. She wore a short-sleeve cardigan over a long dress and a pair of flip-flops. What was it with Americans wearing their flip-flops everywhere?

When she saw him, she rose and walked to the aft, far from the other passengers. Was it to get away from him or for more privacy? As much as he wanted to make a beeline for her, Matias took his time greeting everyone and making small talk with a few of the ladies. There'd still be comments of how he gravitated toward the American woman, and some might even accuse him of giving her more time than anyone else, but it was inevitable.

She glanced in his direction every so often as if to keep stock of his progress on his way to her, and every time she did, he found it harder and harder to pretend her presence didn't affect him.

Why had he offered to take her ashore? It didn't sound like a good idea anymore. They'd be spending time together without the other passengers as a buffer. Already the attraction he had toward her took too much space in his thoughts, and time alone with her only had the likelihood of increasing the attraction. But it was too late to retract the offer, even if he wanted to.

He finally stopped at the railing next to her.

"The weather forecast says it's going to be hot today. You might not need that sweater."

"This is not a fashion statement. It's a necessity to prevent sunburn." She removed her sunglasses and looked up at him. "I wasn't blessed with the golden Portuguese complexion." She dragged one foot against the deck. "Next you're going to tell me I'll trip in my flip-flops."

Matias looked away and scratched the side of his chin.

She chuckled. "I can see that guilty look on your face. Don't deny it."

"I won't confirm or deny anything." He kept a straight face but when he chanced a peek at her, his mouth involuntarily rose in a small smile.

Matias pulled his phone out and checked the time. "Meet me at the reception desk at fifteen past ten."

Her eyebrows scrunched in that expression of hers he was beginning to know better each day. "But the excursion ashore leaves at ten."

"Yes, I know." He resisted the urge to wink at her and stepped back from the railing.

She turned in his direction. "What do you have planned, Captain?"

"You'll just have to wait and see, Miss Clark."

CHAPTER SIX

$\mathcal{V}$anessa arrived at the reception desk a few minutes before the appointed time. The ship was unusually quiet. Most passengers had left in the tour buses heading toward the center of the small town of Régua and the local museum. The schedule called for lunch aboard and another excursion in the afternoon to a seventeenth century palace. Meanwhile, the captain, or perhaps Miguel, would navigate to the next stop and the excursion buses would deliver the passengers to a nearby wine-producing farm for a typical regional dinner before returning everyone to the ship at night. A day full of activities and most likely a low-key evening.

She turned at the sound of muted steps on the carpet. A man in aviator sunglasses walked in her direction. He wore dark jeans and a light blue T-shirt that accentuated his broad shoulders and lean physique in all the right ways. Vanessa stared, trying to remember if she'd seen him around. He smiled and removed his glasses as he approached, and she scolded herself for missing the signs.

"I hardly recognized you out of your uniform, Captain Romano." It shouldn't surprise her that he looked just as good in casual clothes. He probably looked fine in just about anything, but that was a mental picture she did not need right now.

He tucked the sunglasses in the neckline of his shirt, and Vanessa caught herself blushing at the sight of his dark chest hair. Goodness, it was going to be a long day beside this man and whatever he had planned for them. She needed a distraction of another sort— something that didn't spike her internal temperature or make her lose her good sense.

"Not captain. I'm simply Matias for the next few hours."

"Hello, Matias. I'm simply Vanessa," she said in a Barbie-doll tone.

He chuckled. "I have a feeling there's nothing simple about you."

What was that supposed to mean? "I'm not as bad as you think, you know," she defended herself.

The receptionist approached with a backpack, and Matias thanked him. "Relax, Vanessa. It was a compliment." He shouldered the backpack. "Let's just forget about our past animosity toward each other and pretend we can get along like two normal people."

"Whatever you say, cap—Matias," she corrected herself. She didn't even have to pretend. For all the awkward and uncomfortable exchanges between them, he was growing on her at a fast rate. Three days ago she didn't know he existed, and now she was looking forward to a road trip with him.

When they arrived on dock, he walked toward the nearest parking lot and Vanessa followed. He clicked the remote key fob and a candy-apple-red convertible chirped back from under the shade of a large oak tree.

Her eyes widened at the sleek vehicle. "We're driving that?" She hurried on to see the car up close. "It's a Volkswagen. I love Volkswagen cars."

He shook his head slowly. "I asked Miguel to take care of the rental."

She touched the smooth paint. "Don't tell me you don't like it. I've always wanted to drive a red convertible." Her words sounded a bit more wistful than she'd intended.

"So have I." He dropped the backpack in the back seat and went around the front to open the passenger side door to her.

"Will you let me have a turn?" Vanessa rounded the back, appreciating all the fine details. "Please?"

"Sorry, the rental agreement is in my name." He closed the door after she slid onto the smooth leather seat. "Can you even drive a stick shift?"

"It's been a while, but yes, I can." Her first car had been a late eighties jalopy with a lazy starter and a gearstick that stuck at the most inopportune times.

Matias turned on the radio, and started the car, smiling at the soft purr of the engine. "Are you ready?"

Vanessa tied the sun hat under her chin and tucked her low bun more securely, then nodded at him. "Are you going to tell me what we're doing today?"

He kept his eyes on the road. "Do you want me to catch up to the excursion buses?"

"Now you're just being mean." She raised an eyebrow at him. "Of course I don't."

Matias maneuvered through the town center and stopped at a red light. He had a nonchalant hand on the wheel and his elbow on the lowered window, and Vanessa hadn't seen him this relaxed on the ship. Being ashore looked good on him. Her eyes kept straying to him, and he'd reward her with that half smile of his that she liked more and more.

She turned to look out the passenger-side window. As the breeze shifted, Vanessa pushed the sun hat farther down her forehead and kept a hand on it until Matias rounded another curve on the road. The landscape of rolling hills and small farms cascaded to the river in horizontal rows of various greens and fertile dirt. At the small port, the docked ship loomed large next to the smaller one-day cruise ships in the vicinity.

Once they reached the outside of town, Matias pulled over to a side road and parked in a rest area under the shade of linden trees.

He turned off the radio, then reached in the backpack and pulled out a map.

"You're probably wondering why we didn't take the excursion like everybody else, but I realized that it would be really hard to keep track of you among all the others. I also didn't want the regulars asking why I was suddenly taking a trip to shore." He pulled his glasses onto his head and looked at her. "It's something I've never done before, and I don't want to explain why I'm making an exception this time. Besides, I'm sure your grandfather wouldn't want to call undue attention to your situation."

Vanessa took off her sunglasses and untied the hat. "I still think he's blowing everything out of proportion."

"I'm sure he has his reasons," Matias said in a placating voice. "And I'm taking a guess here, but it sounded like he's had bodyguards on you before. You should probably be used to it by now."

"Wow. Assumptions much, Captain?" She leaned away from him and crossed her arms. "Why would you even think that?"

He held up a hand in a surrender gesture. "I'm sorry. I don't want to upset you. Forget I said anything." He waited before adding, "Can you go back to calling me Matias if I don't bring it up again?"

She tapped a finger to her chin and pretended to consider. "How good are you at keeping your promises?"

"Very good—I promise." He didn't even try to keep a straight face.

She wasn't in the mood to argue. "I guess I'll take your word for it," she said in a mock stern voice. "Don't make me regret it."

Matias flashed a smile and picked up the map again. He unfolded it and pointed at a dot.

"This is Régua, where we docked this morning. We're going to bypass the visit to the Museum of the Douro River and drive to the palace near Vila Real. Then we'll drive straight to Pinhão just as the ship docks there and arrive before the buses deliver the passengers so we can avoid any questions about where we went." He turned from the map to look at her. "Is that okay with you?"

"I don't know anything about this area, so it all sounds good to me." Vanessa bent over the map and followed the distance between the places he'd pointed at with her finger. "Will we have the time to drive there and back to the ship?"

Matias added his own finger to the map and traced along with hers, his head leaning close. Vanessa stilled at the proximity. Her heart sped up, and she dared not move. What was this energy again, this feeling of surprising happiness that flushed her face and filled her chest?

He went on, as if unaware of the effect of his nearness. "We'll go north on this road to reach the palace and then southeast on the way back to the ship. Nobody will even know we were gone."

As he smoothed a wrinkle on the map and tried to fold it, Matias bumped her shoulder and knocked her sun hat off her head onto the backseat. His right arm reached out to catch the hat and Vanessa leaned in the wrong direction, bridging the few inches between them. Matias locked eyes on her and, just as she had, he froze for a moment. Neither spoke.

How easily could she touch her lips to his?

A car horn blared from the nearby road.

Vanessa leaned back against her seat, and Matias cleared his throat. She turned partially to the window and sighed, grateful for the timely interruption that had prevented an embarrassing situation.

What was she thinking? She'd been ready to kiss Captain Matias Romano. A kiss, for goodness' sake. And the man worked for Grandfather. A double disaster narrowly missed.

He retrieved the hat and handed it to her. "We should get going."

She placed it on her lap and gave him a small nod.

The key turned easily in the ignition, his touch quick and his hands moving firmly to grip the wheel. After waiting for a break in the traffic, Matias merged onto the road without a glance in her direction.

She probably deserved it.

He'd been ready to kiss her.

Matias gave himself a mental slap for the almost slip-up. No wonder Vanessa had turned to the window. She'd probably seen his intentions written on his face and hadn't wanted to deal with him. He couldn't blame her. He didn't want to deal with himself or the situation either.

He flipped the radio on again and turned the volume on high. The speed limit on the national road was lower than on the highway, but it still made it hard to talk. One of the disadvantages of a convertible car. He'd apologize to her later and hopefully she wouldn't hold it against him. They definitely didn't need any extra tension between them.

As many times as he'd docked at the port of Régua before, he'd only made it as far as the local hotel, and he'd never been to Vila Real before. When was the last time he'd taken a road trip anyway? Nothing came up in recent memory. He always stuck to the cruise itinerary and never had a reason to go ashore. It was about time he changed his routine, even if it hadn't been his idea. The smooth ride and comfortable car would soon have them at the palace, where he could take Vanessa on a walking tour of the beautiful gardens and ask her to forgive his earlier behavior. He'd make new memories, and she would be a part of them. And the next time he came this way, he'd think fondly of their time together. A sense of contentment rose in his chest. It was a good plan.

The car lurched forward to the right side and Matias gripped the wheel. Both he and Vanessa jerked in their seats and he gulped in a breath when the seatbelt held him back. She gasped and snapped her face to him, but he kept his eyes ahead. His hands tightened around the wheel and his knuckles turned white as he gradually decreased the speed and maneuvered to the side of the road. Slowly, he inched the car forward until it safely stopped on the shoulder.

Matias turned off the ignition and leaned back against the headrest, closing his eyes for a moment. The episode had taken only a few seconds, but it had felt much longer.

"What happened?" Vanessa asked.

"I'm pretty sure that was a tire gone flat." He straightened and looked at her. "Are you okay?" She nodded at him and brushed some stray hair out of her face, not completely convincing him.

Before he gave in to the urge to hug her, Matias undid the seatbelt and exited the car. "I'm sorry if that scared you." He bent by the front tire on the driver side, then moved to the back tire.

The sound of a car door opening and closing reached him.

"I think it's this one," Vanessa said.

He came around to her side, where the front tire lay flat on the dirt. "Completely flat," he added unnecessarily. It was beyond saving. He should have known something was coming. Everything had been going so well, but the ill luck had followed them ashore.

Vanessa reached for her hat in the back seat and then stepped next to him. "It happened so fast. How did you know what to do?"

"*Cars*," he replied before thinking.

"What cars?"

Matias took a step back, looking for shade. "The movie *Cars*." At her puzzled expression, he added, "The Disney Pixar movie. You know, the computer-animated one where all the cars act like people."

"You watch animated children's movies?" Then her eyes widened. "Oh my gosh, are you married with kids?"

He stopped. "What? No, of course not." Did she really think he'd be out with her if he were married? "They're my cousin's kids, my cousin Vicente Silva. We get together during the low season."

She shook her head. "And watching that movie told you what to do?"

Maybe not exactly, now that he thought about it. "I guess I was just trying to channel my inner Lightning McQueen—keep my cool and not wreck the car." He walked to the back of the car and lifted the top of the trunk.

"I guess it worked. You didn't wreck the car," she said in a light tone.

Was she mocking him or congratulating him? Matias peeked from behind the back of the car and flashed her a smile. "I always do my best."

The closest tree wasn't close enough to provide shade while he changed the tire. "Vanessa, go ahead and put the car in neutral. I want to roll it under that tree over there."

"Are you sure you want me to sit behind the wheel? I'm not on the rental agreement, remember?" She opened the door but didn't move to sit inside.

Matias swung open the passenger-side door and positioned himself to push. "Haha, very funny," he said flatly. When she still didn't move, he motioned with his head to the driver seat. "Just put it in neutral and steer it to the right. Please," he added.

She slid in and ran her hands along the steering wheel, a smile on her face.

"Come on, Vanessa. The sooner I change the tire, the sooner we can get back on the road."

She nodded and released the brake. After a few pushes and some grunts, Matias got the car close enough to the shade of the large tree. It wasn't perfect, but it would have to do.

He walked to the back of the car and removed the spare tire and the jack from under the mat on the bottom of the trunk and set them on the dirt. After looking around in the trunk again, he found a small zippered pouch with the tools needed for the task.

"What can I do to help?" Vanessa moved closer to his side.

Matias knelt on the dirt and removed the wheel cover. "It's okay. I got this."

She crossed her arms. "I heard about how macho Portuguese men are, but now I'm experiencing it in person. What a treat," she deadpanned. "Matias, I know how to change a tire. I've been changing my own tires since I was sixteen."

He loosened the last lug nut and stopped to look at her. "I'm sure you can change a tire just fine, but I'll do it quicker working by myself."

As he reached for the jack, Vanessa went around the front of the car with a rock in her hands. She dropped it on the dirt and then gave it a few short kicks.

Wheel wedges. Good thinking. He'd forgotten about those. Matias flashed her a thumbs-up sign but she came back around with her arms crossed again.

"Is that what you tell your crew, that you work better alone?"

That was hardly the same thing at all but if he told her that, she'd most likely disagree. He tried a different tactic. "Who taught you how to change a tire?" He raised the car slowly, watching the jack for signs of strain and weakness. "Your father or one of your grandfather's chauffeurs?"

She raised her hands in a surrender gesture and walked off to sit under another tree.

"What?" She didn't reply. "Vanessa, what did I say?" he insisted.

She gestured at the car and didn't say anything. Clearly, he'd said something to make her mad but he couldn't even begin to guess what.

After changing the tire and stowing everything away, Matias called Miguel and apprised him of the situation, promising to keep him updated of their progress. Then he rummaged in the backpack for water bottles. He walked over to Vanessa and handed her one, then sat next to her and uncapped his bottle.

"We can go whenever you're ready," he said to her after drinking half his bottle.

She put down her hat beside her and took little sips from her bottle.

"I'm sorry I upset you, Vanessa."

"Do you even know what you're apologizing for?" she finally asked.

His father used to say *apologize first, understand later*, but maybe that wasn't enough. "Something I said?" He shrugged.

Vanessa looked at him. "Matias, what do you know about me?" She kept her eyes on him. "Other than where I come from and who my Grandfather is."

He couldn't look away from her, from the intensity in her green eyes. For reasons he didn't know, his reply was important to her. This was not the time to be light and flippant.

"Will you tell me more about you?" He added as much sincerity to the words as he could, hoping it was enough to let her see how much he really wanted to know her better, how much he cared.

Something passed through her eyes and, for a moment, he couldn't tell what she wanted to do.

All he had was the earnestness in his own expression, hoping it was enough to sway her.

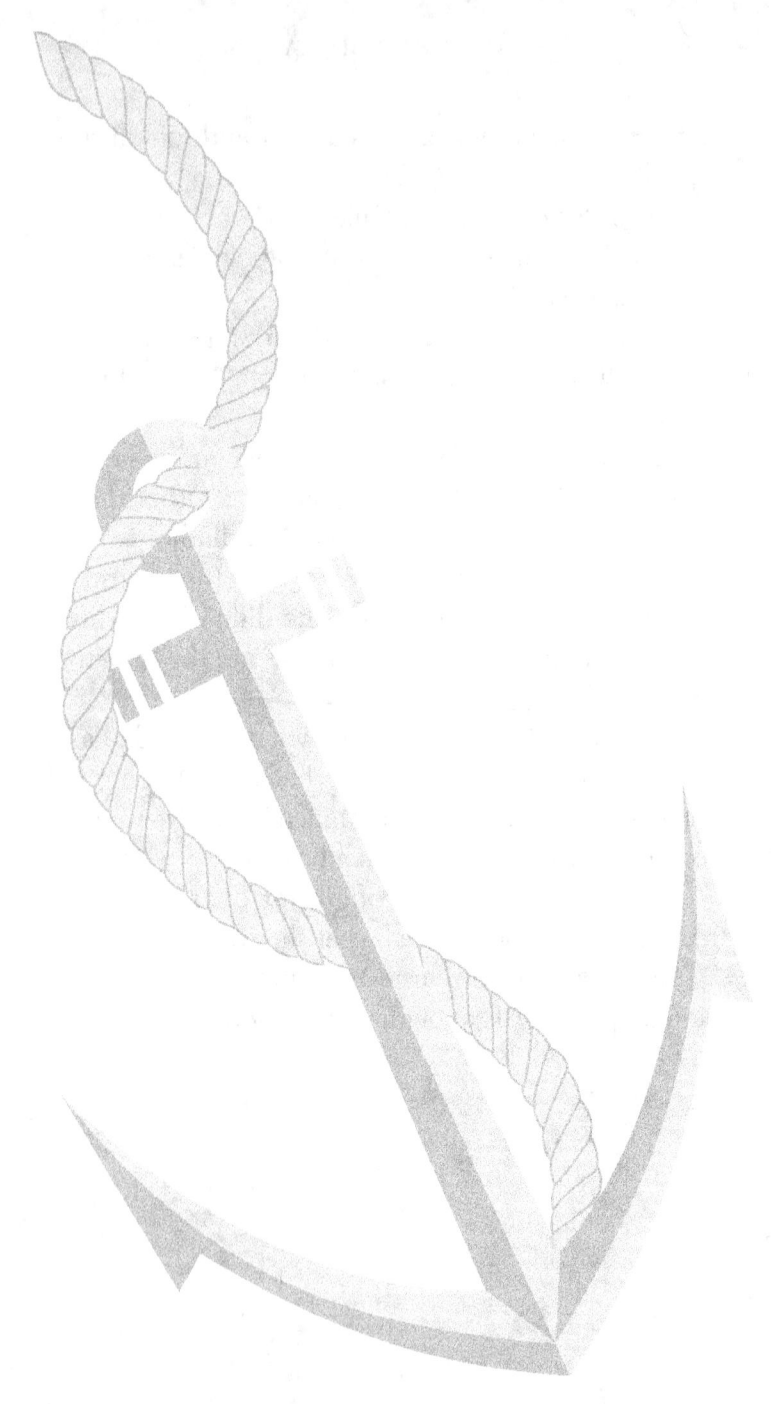

CHAPTER SEVEN

Vanessa sighed and looked away from him. Maybe she'd regret it later, but she wanted him to know.

"I was sixteen and had my car for five months when I had my first flat," she started. "I didn't have a spare and had to leave the car on the side of the road. It took me almost two days before I was able to trade for a spare. I ran down to the library and after reading how to change a tire for twenty minutes, I finally convinced Mrs. Lebowsky to print the instructions off the Internet." Vanessa had kept that folded page in the glove box until the ink had faded off.

"Dad was mad when he found out, but I wanted to be independent. Unfortunately for me, that car proved to have a lot of other problems with the starter and the gearstick. I had to plan my trips to the store and ask someone to come with me in case it got stuck. Then I'd put it in neutral while the person that came with me gave it a running push."

Matias smiled wide. "And that worked?"

"Apart from being humiliating, it worked pretty well. It got more complicated when I couldn't find anyone to come with me. Then I had to park on a downhill slope so I could give it push, then jump in and start it.

"At least you didn't have any witnesses."

"True, but do you know how hard it is to find an incline in Kansas?"

Matias laughed.

"I changed the tires so often, pretty soon I had a record time. My friend Juliette convinced me to bet against the boys from Pete's Garage downtown, and I won." She won the bet pot of $500 dollars. After that, word got out and nobody would dare go against her again. Dad wasn't too happy about it either.

Matias whistled, and she laughed. "It's been a while now, so I'm probably rusty." She sobered. "And that's how I know how to change a tire. Dad didn't teach me, and Grandfather's drivers didn't either."

The high sun grew hot in the approaching lunch hour, and the shadows shrunk closer to their objects. Even the shade of a large tree was not enough any-more, and Vanessa shifted to where the shade touched that of a neighboring tree. Several cars honked by in succession, the first one decorated with ribbons of white tulle.

Matias followed her gaze and waved back at the occupants. "A wedding party on its way to the reception."

After the cars passed, he took a last swig of his water, and then held on to the water bottle, his forehead wrinkled as he processed what she'd told him. "But your grandfather—"

"He's rich. I know." Vanessa nodded at him. "You can't reconcile what you just heard with what you know of Grandfather and me." She shrugged. "That's okay. I still have a hard time understanding it myself."

"How then?"

"It's a long story." She pulled her knees up and wrapped her arms around them. "A pretty unbelievable one." She hadn't told her few friends back home—apart from Juliette. She'd been unable to admit how her own dad had never told her the truth about her past. And here she was now, about to tell it to a stranger. How would he react?

She grabbed the rest of her courage and inhaled a quick breath. "I found out I had a Portuguese grandfather on my twenty-first birthday."

Matias held a hand up. "Hold on. Twenty-first birthday? How old are you?"

"Twenty-three, well on the way to twenty-four."

His eyes widened. "Twenty-three?" he repeated. "I thought you were twenty, twenty-one at the most. Are you done with school then?"

Vanessa nodded. "I graduated two years ago. And how old are you?" She'd been curious about his age since the first day she met him.

"I turned thirty-one last month." He picked up a short stick from the ground and fiddled with it.

"There's less of an age difference between us than I thought."

She drank the last of her water, then capped the bottle and set it aside. "So this whole time you thought I was a young, spoiled, rich girl, didn't you?"

"I did—I mean no." He shook his head. "I did have wrong assumptions about you, and I'm sorry for that. But you were telling me about meeting your grandfather when you turned twenty-one, and I interrupted you. I'm sorry. Please, go on."

He was redirecting the conversation but Vanessa let it go for now. She would find another chance to get to talk about the assumptions he'd made about her.

"I didn't actually meet him on my birthday." She sighed. The memories of her twenty-first birthday still evoked too much confusion, even after two and a half years. "He sent his assistant with an iPad to set up a Skype visit. I didn't even know I had family in Portugal. My dad had told me my mom had died when I was three years old, but he never told me anything else about her."

Vanessa had mistaken Dad's silence for pain and, through the years, hadn't wanted to bring the subject up, even when she had questions. "I mean, look at me." She turned her hands toward herself. "Do I look like I have Portuguese blood? You'd think the dark genes were stronger, but no, Dad's Scandinavian ancestry won out." Her hair was light and her skin sunburned easily. Sometimes she was jealous of the golden glow that Portuguese women owned so effortlessly, of their beautiful, dark eyes and petite, graceful features. So unlike her own.

Matias's mouth turned in a small smile, and he watched her, as if paying attention to her for the first time. His expression softened, and Vanessa looked out to the road, unable to sustain the eye contact. She was blushing again, and he'd be able to see it.

"I do have her nose," she said softly. "My mom's, I mean. It was obvious when I finally saw a picture of her." She touched the tip of her nose, the one she'd never much liked before. "My Portuguese nose on my not-so-Portuguese face."

"What else did you find out about your mother?"

She hesitated. "I—I don't know. I haven't asked much about her yet."

"But all this time, you've never known anything about her. And now you can find out anything you want from someone who knew her personally. Aren't you even a little curious?" Matias asked.

Yes, of course she was curious. But curiosity and courage didn't always go hand in hand, did they? She shrugged in reply, unable to explain all the conflicting emotions she had about her family.

"Why did your grandfather wait so long to contact you?"

She blew out a breath. "Apparently that was my dad's doing. He didn't want Grandfather to"—she made air quotes with her fingers and dragged the word—"*interfere* with me when I was younger. So he waited until I was twenty-one and legally able

81

to make my own decisions. And then Grandfather wanted me to leave everything behind and come live with him in Porto, so he could train me to take over the company when he retires."

"Whoa," Matias said. "That's just—"

"Messed up. I know. Can you imagine? Surprise, you're an heiress. I'm your millionaire grandfather. Come live with me in my mansion." She glanced at Matias. "Insane, right?"

"I can't even imagine. What did you tell him?"

"I told him thank you, but no thank you."

"I bet he didn't like that."

"What did he expect? I'd just graduated and accepted an offer to work with the county for an IT job, and had signed a lease on a new apartment. Of course I wasn't going to move to Porto." Her words came too fast and jumbled, and she inhaled at the end. She should be able to talk about this without getting all riled up by now, but maybe it would be one of those sensitive topics that never lost its sting.

Matias leaned in her direction. "But you're here now."

She shrugged. "That was a compromise of sorts so he would leave me alone for a while. I told him I had a two-year contract and I might be able to take some time off when it was up for renewal. But I made it clear I'd come only for a visit."

"And the cruise?"

"The cruise." She rolled her eyes and Matias smiled. "He wanted me to take the cruise so I could see what his company is all about. He said if I don't change my mind after being on the ship and seeing all the beautiful sights and places, then I can go back, and he won't bother me again."

"Ah," Matias said.

"Ah what?" She watched him closely. "He asked you to change my mind, didn't he?" She wouldn't put it past Grandfather to ask the captain to sway her decision.

He shook his head but didn't immediately meet her eyes. "No. He only asked me to make sure you had a lovely experience. Well, that was before you went on your own yesterday. Then he asked me to keep an eye on you."

"You mean, he asked you to babysit me. And you thought I was a spoiled brat who needed more than a babysitter." It all made sense now. She eyed him sideways. "I'm surprised you didn't try to pawn me off onto one of your assistants."

"No, Vanessa, it's not like that." This time he rested his hand on hers.

Her skin broke in gooseflesh despite the hot temperatures around them, and Vanessa stilled at the something that charged between them, strong and strumming and so unexpected.

His thumb stroked the skin on her inner wrist before he let go. "I'm sorry for the assumptions I made of you. I was wrong, and I had no right to judge you." He paused, his eyes still locked on her. "But I'm not sorry to be here with you, and I'm glad he didn't send the bodyguard."

He meant it. His expression was genuine, and she knew he meant it.

Vanessa stood quickly and walked over to the next tree, rubbing the spot where Matias had touched her, wishing he'd lingered there for a while longer. Such a crazy, unexpected wish.

She was attracted to the captain and she wouldn't be doing anything about it. Something else to add to the confusing mess that was her life since António Valadares had come into it.

Matias came beside her and handed her the hat. "What plans—"

"I think we should get moving," she interrupted him. "Will that spare be enough to get us to where we're going?" She replaced the hat on her head and put on her sunglasses.

Matias dropped the empty bottles inside the back-pack, then opened the passenger door for her. "No, it won't. We'll have to stop at the next town."

"Do you need to call someone and tell them what happened?"

"I already told Miguel what's going on."

"Anyone else you need to call?" Maybe he wasn't married, but he might have someone else he'd keep informed of his whereabouts. After all, this outing wasn't a date, but an assignment from Grandfather.

He raised an eyebrow. "No, I don't have to call anyone else."

She pulled the seat belt across her lap.

He sat behind the wheel, his fingers hovered on the ignition. "Vanessa—"

She put on a pleasant expression, ready to change the subject to a less personal one. "It's okay, Matias. Let's just go."

Matias pulled the small car to the far edge of the parking lot near the dock and turned off the ignition. The ship sat quiet, with a gentle glow from the floodlights against the darkness of the river behind it.

He and Vanessa were finally back. What a day.

He'd had a simple plan: take a drive to the palace, spend an hour touring the gardens, have lunch, and drive back to meet the ship at the next port. That way Vanessa could have her excursion ashore, and he could keep an eye on her as he'd promised her grandfather.

But he should have known better than to hope for everything to go well. He'd had problems aboard even before departure, and the problems had followed him to land as well. The flat tire had been bad luck, further aggravated by a lack of the special tire brand they needed at the three garages they'd called at, and the long, long wait for a new rental car to arrive.

Matias sighed and rolled his shoulders. He turned to Vanessa, slumped against her seat and breathing softly in her sleep, her expression relaxed and pleasing. Her hair had since fallen out of its bun and curled around her cheeks and neck. Despite her wearing the oversized sun hat all day, her nose had pinked a little brighter than the rest of her face. She probably wouldn't like, it but the rosy tone looked good on her.

Vanessa's words about her family situation still swirled in his mind; he was unable to let go of them easily. He had so many questions. So many he wanted to ask her. And why wasn't she asking any to her grandfather? There had to be more at stake than just general confusion on her part. Between a dead mother, a father who'd kept vital secrets, and a grandfather who wanted her only for what she could give him, the whole situation was bizarre. He understood how everything affected Vanessa's willingness to delve into her past. She was afraid and unwilling to find out what she needed, but her fear kept her from getting the answers that could help her move on.

He nudged her. "Vanessa, we're here." When she didn't move, he touched her arm again. "Come on, Vanessa, wake up. We need to go aboard."

She opened her eyes and sat up slowly. "Matias," she said in a low voice.

The little way she said his name—with a Z sound at the end instead of the Portuguese pronunciation—was how he liked to hear it.

He waited a few minutes for her to orient herself. "Hey there. Did you have a nice nap?" he teased.

"I was supposed to keep you company, not fall

asleep." She brushed the stray hair away. "Is that the ship ahead?"

She exited the car, and he came around to meet her. "It took a while, but we made it."

"It wasn't so bad, was it? I actually enjoyed myself," Vanessa said, her eyes still on the ship. "I know you were worried because we missed the visit to the palace and the second car took forever to arrive, but it was a fun day." She paused for a moment, then added. "With you. I had fun with you."

"You're right. It was a fun day." Maybe his plans hadn't worked out, but being with her had made everything better. "Thanks for being a good sport about everything."

Her eyebrows rose in a mischievous expression, and she bumped his elbow. "You're just glad I didn't throw a fit. Since I'm a spoiled brat and all that." She held her hat by the brim and walked off ahead of him.

That was not what he'd thought of her, but the right words didn't come to him.

When he didn't follow her, she turned around. "Come on, Captain, let's get you back to your ship."

Miguel waited for them at the gangway. "Welcome back, Captain."

"Thanks, Miguel. It's good to be back."

"Miss Clark." Miguel nodded in her direction.

"Hi, Miguel. Did you miss us?" she asked in a playful tone.

"I'm just glad to see you both aboard safe and sound."

"I couldn't agree more," Matias said.

A few passengers sat in the lounge, but the ship was otherwise quiet at the late hour. Relieved, Matias followed Vanessa to the reception area, where they stopped before parting ways. Her cabin was down the hall to the bow side and his was two decks lower, almost exactly below.

"Thanks for taking me ashore, Matias," she said.

"You're welcome." He cringed inside. After everything that went wrong, she still thanked him. "I'm sorry you didn't get to see the gardens at the palace."

She shrugged with a small smile, then waved at him before walking down the hall.

"Vanessa," he called after her. "Do yourself a favor and sleep in tomorrow."

She cocked her head. "But then I'd miss the sunrise with you."

CHAPTER EIGHT

*V*anessa stretched in bed and yawned. Through the partly drawn curtains, the pale light of the early sun fell on the carpeted floor. Her cabin faced the port side with a view of the small town of Pinhão. She hadn't seen much of it last night, having arrived after dark and after an uncomfortable nap in the small car. Although the trip hadn't lived up to their expectations, the company had made up for the lack of activities and Matias had proved himself to be both entertaining and a great listener. She hadn't planned to tell him so much about her past and the reasons for the strained relationship with Grandfather, but at least now he knew where she came from.

When she turned to check the time on the bedside table clock, a white piece of paper on the floor by the door drew her attention. Vanessa rose and picked up a square envelope with her name written on the

front in straight block letters. Inside was a card in
the ship's stationery, the company logo preceding
a short message:

> *Vanessa,*
> *Please meet me at the reception desk at eleven a.m.*
> *Dress in comfortable clothes and sturdy shoes, and*
> *bring your sun hat and sunscreen.*
> *We'll be taking a trip into the past.*
> *M.R.*

A note from the captain about a trip into the past.
She didn't like to look into the past; it didn't usually
bring good things. Hopefully he meant there was
a visit to some historical place planned for the excursion ashore today, and not another talk where she
spilled her family secrets.

Vanessa stood for a minute, appreciating the strong
handwriting, decidedly masculine and confident. She
touched the smooth paper and traced the signature,
then brought the letter to her nose and smelled it.
When she caught her reflection on the mirror behind
the door, Vanessa pulled the card away and shoved
it inside the drawer on the bedside table. What was
she doing, hoping to get a whiff of Matias's cologne?
Pathetic. Before she fell to the urge to do it again,
Vanessa opened the closet and picked a floral dress
to wear for breakfast, then entered the bathroom for
a quick shower.

She'd missed the early breakfast in the lounge,
and the dining room was full of passengers already

seated and others piling their plates at the buffet. The cruise director stood at the far end of the room with a clipboard in her hands, talking to Miguel and another female crew member. Vanessa looked around the room twice but didn't see Matias and guessed he must be at the bridge.

Someone touched her arm and Vanessa turned to find Agnes Grantham's smiling face.

"Vanessa, how are you, dear? I didn't see you yesterday."

Mr. Grantham excused himself and exited the room toward the hallway.

Vanessa smiled at the older lady. "How are you, Agnes?"

"Are you joining us for the excursion today?"

Vanessa hesitated. Matias hadn't told her to keep their trips a secret, but they didn't want others to know why she needed a sort of bodyguard to accompany her ashore.

Mrs. Grantham winked at her. "I see that you already have other plans. Have a fun day! And don't forget the barbecue tonight," she added over her shoulder.

She left with a wave before Vanessa had the chance to reply. Had Agnes seen Vanessa and Matias return from their trip? It was possible that the passengers whose cabins faced the port side had witnessed their arrival last night.

After breakfast, Vanessa returned to her cabin. The bed had been made, the bathroom cleaned, and the towels changed. There wasn't much to do, and she still had some time before meeting Matias. She sat on the side of the bed and looked around the beautifully decorated cabin.

She missed the busyness of her life in Osawatomie, Kansas, her days filled with purpose and a job to do, her weekends working for the county emergency response team. Dad lived in Kansas City, where she'd grown up, and even though the relationship had been strained between them the past couple of years, they talked on the phone weekly and met for lunch once or twice a month.

Her group of friends from college was still in contact, pushing Vanessa to date more often. She'd sworn off dating for a while after Jason, the fireman. Better alone than in bad company, she'd told her friends, but they insisted she keep trying. What would they say if they knew of her day trips with Captain Matias Romano? She hadn't updated her Facebook page since the first day of the trip and didn't feel the need to now.

Here, what she knew as normal was suspended, out of routine. Vacations were supposed to be a time away from the ordinary, a time of discovery and learning, or fun and relaxation. But this trip to Portugal was fraught with tension, with Dad's texts and calls coming in more often than she'd like and Grandfather's plans always in the back of her mind. She'd refused his proposal, and she kept her return plane ticket next to her passport. But after the ship returned to port at the end of the trip, she still had one more week in Porto, and she didn't know what Grandfather and Grandmother had planned for her last days in the country. Whatever the case, she was not ready for a confrontation with him, and she'd rather not see the rest of the family again.

Out on the dock, the tour buses honked. Vanessa stood from the bed and parted the curtains, opening the sliding doors to the balcony to watch the passengers board. As fun as it looked, she was looking forward to taking a private excursion with Matias instead of going in the buses with the others.

Her heart sped up at the thought of their time together and she bit her lip as a half smile bloomed there.

Today would go well.

"Is that where we're going?" Vanessa asked. Her voice pitched higher with excitement, and she cleared her throat to disguise it.

A medieval-looking village with round turrets and other buildings perched on a hill a few short miles down the road. She leaned forward to get a better view.

Matias glanced at her from behind the wheel and nodded with a smile. "It's great, isn't it?" He turned off the engine and set the parking break. "I'll be right back." He disappeared inside the front door of a roadside building.

Vanessa exited the car as well and held her smart-phone to take a picture of their destination. When she turned around, she chuckled lightly at Matias's choice of car for today.

"I saw that," Matias said as he came out of the café with a large basket in his hands. "I told you earlier, I know this beige Ford Escort is not as exciting as the red Volkswagen convertible we had yesterday, but at least the tires are the most common everywhere and we won't be stranded if we have another flat." He opened the trunk and stowed the basket inside.

Vanessa stepped closer to him to take a peek, unable to hold back her curiosity. "Is that a picnic basket?"

Matias locked the trunk and grinned at her. "What if I say yes?"

She grinned back, her heart beating a little faster, as he led her to the passenger seat, then went around the front to his side.

An outdoor picnic. At a medieval village.

Her hands shook a little, and she laced her fingers on her lap. "Promise not to laugh if I tell you something." For a moment, she regretted the statement. It was a silly dream from her childhood.

Matias pulled back into the road. "What is it? I promise not to laugh," he added in response to her silence.

Vanessa inhaled a quick breath and looked on ahead, unable to see Matias watch her every now and then while he drove. "When I was a little girl

I always wanted to have a picnic under a tree overlooking a castle." In her young mind, the castle from her imagination resembled the Cinderella one from Disney World, but the medieval village at the end of the road was much better.

His expression relaxed in a wide smile. "For the record, I'm not laughing, I'm smiling." He turned on the blinker and exited the main road.

"What are you doing?" Her smile vanished. "I thought we were going to see the castle ruins."

"We'll get there, but I'm hungry." He glanced at her, the smile still on his face. "I think I'd like to have a picnic first. Besides, the tour buses are still at Castelo Rodrigo, and I'd rather not meet any of the passengers there. They'll be leaving to the restaurant soon."

And then she and Matias could go to the village and avoid meeting the excursion. "Sounds perfect to me."

After a few turns, he took a secondary road until they came to a clearing on one side and a row of sparse olive trees on the other. Matias parked at the mouth of the clearing and handed her a blanket while he carried the basket. They took a foot path on the beaten dirt until they reached a large olive tree. Vanessa spread the blanket in the shade and sat down near the corner.

A high sun cast the shadows straight down on them. Vanessa adjusted her sun hat and breathed a contended sigh. The scent of summer clung to the air, heavy with sun-baked earth and half-dried grass.

In the wild bushes, the rustle of insect wings buzzing between the tiny yellow flowers played the background soundtrack to a landscape largely untouched by the passage of time and the interference of man. Nary a breeze whispered through the dark leaves and ripe fruit in the wide branches above, and it was hard to believe the river flowed to the north, less than thirty minutes away. Beside her, Matias removed the items from the basket.

He handed her a water bottle. "A tree, a picnic, and a castle on the hill." He leaned back against the tree trunk and crossed his ankles. "Will this do?"

"It will do very well." She turned from watching the view and looked at him. "Thank you."

"Much better than staying on the side of the road with a flat tire, isn't it?"

She nodded. "Thanks for renting a boring car, Matias."

He chuckled. "My pleasure." He passed a plate to her. "Help yourself, please."

When her phone rang, Vanessa suppressed a groan. She reached in her pocket, took it out, and turned it off. "Sorry about that. I forgot to turn it off."

"Do you need to take the call?"

"No, it's just Dad. I can talk to him later." She'd send him a text when they returned to the ship.

"Are you sure? He's calling from the United States, right?"

"Yes, I'm sure." She gestured at the picnic. "So what do we have here?"

"Just a small sample of local foods." Matias pointed at each item. "White and dark artisan bread, traditional smoked ham, cured cheese and fresh cheese from sheep's milk, red grapes, black and green olives, fresh black figs, peach jam, and raw honey."

"My goodness, you call this a small sample? You went all out. And then you expect me to hike to that village on the hill after all this?"

"You'll need your strength," he said to her in between bites.

"I'll need a stroller to carry me around."

"No, I'm pretty sure you'll have to push me," he said in a teasing tone.

Vanessa pointed at a fig. "What do these taste like? I've had Fig Newtons but not real figs."

Matias picked a fig and peeled back the skin halfway. "Yes, these are real figs." He handed it to her. "Emphasis on real. Fig Newtons are definitely not figs. They're more like sorry excuses."

Vanessa took a tentative bite. "The flavor is mild, but it has so many little seeds."

"You eat the whole fig, Vanessa." He popped one in his mouth. "You don't even need to peel it back, but some people don't like the skin. The ancient Greeks considered figs to be the food of the gods, you know."

She reached for a piece of bread and a slice of meat. "I'll take your word for it."

Matias reached for another fig. "When I was a kid, all the family would go help at my grandparents' farm at this time of year. The boy cousins had the job of climbing the fig trees and the girl cousins were supposed to catch the figs that didn't make it to the baskets, but us boys would just stay up there and eat the fruit instead."

His lips curved in a smile, and the playful memory brought out the boy in him. Vanessa could almost see the child he'd been then. "I bet you were one of the instigators."

He chuckled. "Every chance I got. I wasn't the oldest, but I sure knew how to get us all in trouble."

"And when did you change your wayward ways?" Some time along the way, he'd grown into a responsible adult.

His expression faltered, but he caught himself and smiled wanly, sadness replacing his easy manner.

"My mother had cancer when I was thirteen," he said after a pause.

"I'm sorry, Matias. Is she okay now?"

"She is, but it was a hard year for my family. It taught me to sober up and be someone my parents could count on." His voice was wistful. "Even my cousins learned to dial back, and we began to express ourselves with more worthwhile activities. At least for a while." He smiled. "I took my first job on a boat when I was fourteen."

The experience of his mother's illness had shaped him. "Your parents didn't oppose?"

He shrugged. "Boats are what the family does. My father and all his brothers and other extended family. The only difference is they do fishing or small merchandise and I ended up in a cruise ship instead."

In a way, her Portuguese family was similar, with Grandfather's fleet and a few of the cousins taking jobs in the ships and the hospitality business. Grandmother had remarked about who did what, but Vanessa couldn't remember the details. "So all the men in your family take to the river and the women don't mind?"

Matias plucked a blade of dry grass and twirled it between his fingers. "I think they're used to it by now. I certainly have never heard anyone complaining."

"Maybe they complain behind the mens' backs and you just don't know it." All that time away didn't sit right with her. "And you say that because you're not married."

He paused to consider. "Would you mind being married to someone who worked in the river?" His expression wasn't completely serious but his eyes locked on her.

The question surprised her. It bordered on intimate, and she didn't know what to reply.

After a moment, Matias reached for a cluster of grapes and commented on the many varieties that were cultivated in the region.

He'd evaded her personal questions but this time she didn't want to talk about the subject of marriage either, and the change of topic was welcome.

They spent the next half hour eating and discussing the benefits of locally sourced food, and when they were done they packed the leftovers in the basket.

Matias drove back to the main road, and they left the car parked in the narrow shade of a high wall at the foothills of the village.

"Tell me about this place," Vanessa asked Matias as they hiked to one of the arched entrances. "What's it called?"

"Castelo Rodrigo. It's an official stop on the route of historical Portuguese villages because of its significance to the region and importance in the defense against the invasion of Moors and Spaniards." He stopped and pointed at a row of blue and white tiles depicting the main buildings in the village.

Up here the air smelled of sweet honey and almonds, a local treat curiously advertised on the backs of life-size cutouts of donkeys. Vanessa and Matias pondered its meaning but let it go when every plausible explanation failed.

They strolled the narrow cobbled streets, the houses and buildings made of the same dark-yellow stones as the irregular ones paving the ground. Matias pointed out details of a distant past: a Jewish inscription on the lintel stone over a door, a millstone embedded in a house façade, a medieval cistern that saved rainwater for times when the village lay under siege. He told her a few of the facts and stories, and even a legend that made her smile.

Terra-cotta pots adorned windows and doors with bright flowers and native shrubs, and Matias greeted the few locals they passed, often engaging with them for a few moments while Vanessa mangled a Portuguese word or two she'd learned since arriving in the country. It was such a hard language.

Vanessa watched the expression on Matias's face as he talked; she listened to his calm, deep voice, and a feeling unfamiliar to her nestled in her chest and warmed her heart. How could a place she'd never visited before bring such contentment?

Everywhere she walked, the weight of the past was visible in its effect on the present.

"The past is alive here," she said as they watched the view of the valley below from the highest point on the castle ruins.

"The past is alive everywhere, only more evident here." Matias replied. "It's hard to hide the mistakes of men when even the rocks stand as a testament to their actions." He stepped forward to the window opening of an exterior wall in ruins. "But people still ignore it and end up making the same mistakes, don't they? That's why it's important we learn as much we can from the generation before us, even when we don't agree with them."

He climbed a set of steps to the roofless interior court, and Vanessa stayed behind. She was one of those people ignoring the past, unwilling as she was to talk to her grandparents. Would she come to regret it? Would she look back one day and wish she'd learned everything she could from them before she no longer had the chance?

"Vanessa, come see." Matias called her to the opposite side.

A family with two teenage boys approached the window where she stood, and Vanessa walked over to Matias.

He gestured to the field. "Look, that's the olive tree where we had the picnic."

It barely looked the same from up here, but she'd want to remember it and the time they'd had together for lunch.

She drew her phone out of her pocket and held it up for a picture.

"Here, let me," he offered, stepping closer.

Vanessa handed him the phone and smiled for the camera.

The father of the family approached and said something in Portuguese to Matias. Matias looked to the guy and then to her. He smiled and replied with a nod, handing him the phone. He walked to Vanessa and stood next to her.

The guy shook his head and said something else at which Matias replied with a laugh. He nodded at the guy, looked at her, then brought his arm around her shoulder in a side hug.

"Say cheese, Vanessa," he whispered close to her ear, a wide smile on his face.

Vanessa stilled. Whether she smiled or not, she couldn't tell. All she knew was the feeling of Matias's warm body next to hers, the shiver it sent down her arm, the warmth that pooled in her middle in a wave of fluttering sensations. This close, his masculine scent was stronger. She turned to look at Matias, and when he met her eyes, her breath caught at the softness she found there.

The guy stepped forward to return the phone, and Matias squeezed her shoulder before letting go of her. They exchanged a few more words, then Matias said goodbye as the man went after his family.

Matias looked at the screen. "That's a keeper."

"What did he say?" Vanessa took the phone back. "What did he say before he took the picture?"

Matias rubbed a hand along his jawline, a crooked smile at the corner of his mouth. "He asked if my girlfriend was mad at me since we were not standing together. When I said no, he told me to get closer to you." He shrugged. "I figured it was easier to do it than explain you're not my girlfriend. Sorry," he added after a short pause.

Vanessa stared at him. "You don't look very sorry to me." He didn't look sorry at all.

"You're right." He nodded. "I'm not sorry." He winked at her.

Maybe she wasn't either.

CHAPTER NINE

$\mathcal{M}$atias grabbed a can of soda from the ice-filled metal tub and popped the tab. He took a long drink as he gazed around at the sun deck from his vantage point by the bridge. In the pre-dusk light, the ship shone brightly with the string lights that had been added to the existing flood lights as decoration for the barbecue.

Chef Teresa and her assistants worked at the two grills that had been brought up from shore for the occasion, one for the meats and the other for fish. Tables had been lined up along the port side and a buffet lain out where the passengers could fill their plates while enjoying the live band playing traditional music under the canopy. The light chatter, smiling faces, and laughter were all the signs Matias needed to know everything was going well tonight.

Since the start of the party, his gaze had followed Vanessa. In between making small talk with the passengers and checking in with the crew, Matias looked for her among the others. Not so overtly as to draw attention to himself, but enough to know her whereabouts on deck. Did his behavior border on stalkerish? He had told her grandfather he'd keep an eye on her, but maybe he didn't need to be so attentive tonight. They were on board, after all, surrounded my passengers he knew well enough and crew he could vouch for. But try as he might, Matias found himself turning his attention to her every few minutes, his eyes gravitating to hers, his pulse racing when he caught her looking at him. The need to exchange words didn't even cross his mind at those moments. Just knowing she was there was enough.

After such a dismal trip yesterday, their outing to Castelo Rodrigo today had been perfect. He would have stayed there all day and evening if given the chance, talking to her and watching her reactions to the places and history they'd come across while exploring the village.

How was he going to stop himself from comparing this trip to all the others that came after? And did he even want to?

Enough thinking about Vanessa. He should be out there mingling with the passengers. Matias threw the empty soda can in the garbage, and as he walked by a small group of passengers, Mrs. Whitehead called him over. She sat nearby with her husband and the Smiths, who'd been on the cruise before.

He greeted them. "How are you doing, Mrs. Whitehead? Enjoying yourself?"

She nodded. "I was just telling Mrs. Smith what a great party this is."

"I think you and your crew outdid yourselves this year, Captain," Mrs. Smith said. "Everything is outstanding. And the trip to Castelo Rodrigo today was excellent. We enjoyed it so much."

Matias smiled. "Thank you. I'll pass your compliments along to Miss Rialto and her assistants." He didn't have much to do with the planning of the excursions ashore and entertainment aboard, but it was always nice to know that the passengers were happy with both.

A collective gasp drew his attention, and Matias turned around. Past the swimming pool, near the stern of the ship, a group of passengers congregated by the railing on the port side. Just as he tried to assess what was going on, the band stopped playing. More gasps and exclamations had several others who stood closer running to the same spot. He took off in the same direction.

A woman's voice yelled "Now!"

When Matias arrived, the passengers parted to let him through. In the center, Mrs. Grantham lay in a chaise lounge, eyes closed, skin pale, her breathing labored and shallow. Her husband knelt by her on one side of the chair, and Vanessa knelt by the other, holding a glass of what looked like orange juice and cradling the lady's neck.

"What's going on?" Matias went down on one knee next to Vanessa.

"Hypoglycemic shock." She kept her eyes on Mrs. Grantham and spoke to her in a soft voice. "Come on, Agnes, little sips."

Some of the juice dribbled down a corner of the Mrs. Grantham's mouth, and her husband wiped it with a handkerchief. Vanessa lifted the glass again and repeated the process.

Matias reached for his phone and called Afonso to the deck, then he asked the passengers to clear the area. The band resumed its playing, this time with a calmer tune. Jaime was already on the walkie-talkie, and within a minute Afonso arrived with the emergency response kit.

Vanessa turned to look at them both, a look of surprise in her expression. "What's he doing here?" She tipped her chin toward Afonso. "Isn't he the pianist?"

"He's also the emergency response specialist. Let him see what he needs, Vanessa."

Mrs. Grantham opened her eyes slowly even though her color was still pale.

Vanessa stepped aside to make room for Afonso. "You'll be okay, Agnes. Just sit here and drink a little more of the orange juice."

When Pedro approached him, Matias asked him to bring the emergency stair chair for transport in preparation for the paramedics. Afonso had taken over the emergency response box and had placed the oxygen mask over Mrs. Grantham's face while listening to the lady's heartbeat with the stethoscope. Vanessa knelt to the side in case he needed assistance. Her earlier actions and response were sure and affirmative, like those of someone with knowledge and authority. What kind of training did she have? She hadn't mentioned anything but the way she talked and acted belied an assurance that went beyond casual interest.

The paramedics arrived and soon had Mrs. Grantham safely removed from the sun deck. Vanessa followed them to the back of the ambulance, offering any support she could to Mr. Grantham. Matias sent a junior crew member, one of the youngest girls, to help assist with translation when the Granthams arrived at the local hospital.

As he stood by the railing, Anabela Rialto returned from talking to the head paramedic just before the ambulance left.

"He said they'll probably keep her in observation for the night," she said.

"Did you see what happened?" Matias asked.

She nodded. "It happened so fast. Miss Clark was talking to the Granthams and the Olivettis near the prow, and suddenly she took Mrs. Grantham by the arm to sit on a lounger. By then you could tell Mrs. Grantham was definitely not feeling well. She was shaking and very pale. At that point, Miss Clark asked for orange juice. Well, actually, she yelled for it."

"I did hear that," Matias said. It had been the urgent tone in Vanessa's voice that alerted him to something out of the ordinary going on.

"Mr. Grantham said his wife has been having blood sugar problems." Miss Rialto continued. "I'm glad Miss Clark was with her and knew what to do. It could have turned out so much worse."

They hadn't had an emergency aboard in quite some time. Protocol demanded rigorous preparation for any sort of eventuality. During the low season, the entire crew received specialty training, but what could have been done to help Mrs. Grantham in such a case? He needed the whole story from Vanessa.

The mood had mellowed on the sun deck. There was still eating and drinking and dancing, but some of the passengers huddled in smaller groups talking among themselves with obvious concern in their expressions. Some pulled Vanessa aside when she came up the stairs, but she didn't stay behind to answer their questions. She looked around the deck until she met his eyes, and Matias excused himself to make his way in her direction.

"Come on, let's go somewhere we can talk," he said when he reached her.

"I was just about to say the same." She leaned in his direction and Matias placed a hand on her back as he led her down, unable to keep his distance from her.

The sooner they could get away from the barbecue and the curious stares of passengers and crew, the better.

Vanessa walked beside Matias until they reached the end of the hallway on the upper deck. He'd placed his hand on her lower back before descending the stairs and the warmth of his fingers persisted, if only a vestige. Every time they met, she wished for more closeness between them and this unexpected reaction confused her. She hadn't come on the cruise to meet a guy, but after the fun day she'd had ashore with Matias, the preoccupation with Grandfather's plans for her had lost its urgency.

But now was not the time to think about her outings with Matias. A passenger had suffered an emergency and he, as the ship's captain, wanted to know what happened. That was the only reason he wanted to see her in private. She was the one thinking of double meanings where there were none.

He opened the sliding doors, and they stepped onto the rear balcony. Here, away from the party and noise and crowd, the night was calm and the moment almost intimate. Vanessa gave herself another mental shake and stepped away from him. He wanted a report—nothing more.

Matias leaned forward on the railing and rested his forearms. "I've been trying to piece together what happened, but it looks like I need to thank you for your quick response."

Across the river, on the other bank, the village lights twinkled in the darkness, and Vanessa kept her focus on them. "It happened fast. I think it was more one of those moments when someone is at the right place and at the right time."

"I'm guessing you have some kind of training." His tone was half question, half declaration, as if he already knew the answer.

"I work a second job as an EMT," she confirmed. "Usually I join the rig on weekends and some holidays. I'm what they call a floater to cover other responders' shifts." She might as well keep busy with something worthwhile. Idleness never was happiness, as Dad used to say.

Matias stepped away from the railing and turned to her. "So during the week you're an IT specialist, and on weekends you're an EMT?"

She arched an eyebrow at him. "Is that so hard to believe?"

Matias held a hand up. "Of course not. Not at all." He opened his mouth as if to say something else but then paused a few moments. "Tell me about Mrs. Grantham. How did you know she was in trouble?"

"While we were talking, I noticed she started sweating along her hairline, her hands were shaking and she turned pale. The symptoms came on suddenly, and I insisted she sit down before she lost consciousness. Then I asked someone for orange juice so we could get her blood sugar up a little."

"Miss Rialto said it could have been much worse if it hadn't been for your quick intervention."

"A hypoglycemic shock is serious. Hopefully she can return aboard tomorrow morning." Vanessa hadn't helped for the attention or to receive thanks. Her training had kicked in when she recognized the symptoms, and she was just glad she'd been able to help. "How is the barbecue going on the sun deck?" Time to talk about something else.

Matias glanced at her sideways, probably catching on to her change in conversation, but he didn't comment on it. "It's going well. It's usually one of the highlights on the cruise for a lot of the passengers. The regional food and wine and the folk music make it different from what we have going paused to look at her. "And you, did you enjoy yourself?"

His tone was cautious, a careful probing. There was more intention behind it than his casual expression gave away, as if he were expecting her to reveal her true self in just a few words.

"I did. The food was excellent and the music—" She inhaled, borrowing time for the perfect word— "invigorating." She laughed lightly.

"Invigorating?" Matias chuckled. "I never thought of it that way, but yes, it is."

"I don't know why I used that word." She shrugged. "Sometimes I say silly things after something serious happens. My dad didn't like it too much when I was growing up. He'd get upset with me." Vanessa cringed inwardly. That was too much to share.

"There's nothing wrong with that. It's just a way to diffuse the tension after a hard situation. Some people use humor, others like to go out for a drink with their friends after work."

"What kind of person are you: go out for drinks or say silly things?"

"I guess a bit of both. I remember going out with my cousins and we'd get silly," he said. "So it was just you and your father growing up? No other family?"

She shook her head. "No one else, just the two of us."

"And you never asked him why?"

"I did a few times, but his answers were plausible, and he always seemed upset when I asked, so I stopped asking."

"And now, how does it feel to know you have grandparents and extended family?"

How could she explain something she still had a hard time with? "It's been hard. I don't know how to react or what to say. When I arrived in Porto, my grandparents had a big welcome dinner for me with all the extended family. There were so many people, and they made me the center of attention. I kind of freaked out and hid in my apartment for the next few days." She cringed at the memory. "They had good intentions, and I should have reacted differently, but there's no manual, you know? I feel like whatever I choose to do, I'll be disappointing someone."

It was easy to think she knew her choice regarding her future and her family ties to Portugal. But the truth was much different when her final decision carried so much weight.

Matias seemed pensive for a moment. "Have you tried talking to your grandfather?"

Vanessa covered her eyes and shook her head. The memory of that disaster was still very clear. "It didn't go so well last time."

The sound of a series of dings interrupted them and Matias grabbed this phone from his pocket and looked at his screen. "Excuse me. I have to take this."

She nodded and took a step back to give him some privacy. That had been a timely interruption, just as the conversation between them had taken a more intimate turn. Why did she always talk so much about herself to Matias? He only had to ask the right questions and she spilled all her secrets. Was she so starved for male attention, or was Matias so easy to talk to? Or maybe it was both.

When she peeked back at him, he was still looking attentively at the screen, his forehead wrinkled with concern.

"I'm sorry. I'm needed on the lower deck," he said when he noticed her.

"Is everything alright?" She raised a hand to her collar bone. "It's not about Mrs. Grantham, is it?" Had the poor lady taken a turn for the worse?

His expression relaxed. "No, nothing like that. Just some maintenance issues that popped up." He opened the sliding doors back to the hallway. "I'll escort you back to the sun deck."

Vanessa passed, and he closed the doors behind them. This time he didn't touch her lower back, and she missed the small gesture. "I think I'm turning in. It's been a long day." She stopped in front of the door to her cabin and Matias stood a few steps ahead.

Was he trying to put more distance between them? Had she said something he didn't like? She reached for her key card and slid it in the electronic lock, then crossed her arms, rubbing her left elbow, the one she'd hit against the side of the lounge chair when she'd helped Mrs. Grantham. She'd been so busy earlier she'd hardly noticed the dull pain.

He slipped his hands in his pockets and looked down the hallway in the direction of the main stairs. "Thanks again for your help today."

"You're welcome."

He waited until she entered her cabin. Vanessa closed the door and leaned against it for a moment.

She closed her eyes and shook her head. That couldn't have been any more awkward.

Why did the possibility of a new relationship always feel so strained? Was there even a chance?

CHAPTER TEN

*M*atias scrubbed his chin and yawned. Another long day drew to a close. He exited the bridge and walked around to the prow. The small town of Barca d'Alva was the port of call tonight, and he faced the river and the reflected lights, twinkling in the flow of the water.

After breakfast, he'd turned the ship around for the trip back while half the passengers had left on a bus for the tour to Salamanca, Spain. Miss Rialto had accompanied them ashore, as she usually did, and one of her assistants had stayed behind to lead the remaining passengers in some deck games.

Throughout the day, he'd had glimpses of Vanessa here and there. The Granthams had returned from the hospital before breakfast, and Vanessa had spent some time with Mrs. Grantham in the lounge. She'd caught his eye and smiled back at him but

Matias had been occupied with charts, reports, and passengers, and only waved from afar.

"You've been busy today, Captain," Vanessa said from behind him.

He'd been so distracted thinking about her, he didn't even notice her approaching. Matias stepped away from the railing, and his mouth curled in a smile. The urge to come closer and hug her took him by surprise. He'd missed seeing her, in more ways than one, but the feeling was stronger than he'd anticipated. After knowing her for only a few days, she filled his mind and heart too much already.

"Good evening, Miss Clark," he said, grinning like a fool. Not knowing what to do with his hands, he slipped them into his pants pockets to prevent himself from touching her.

She wore a floral dress of some gauzy, flowy material—one of those dresses that flattered without clinging. It had Matias itching to hold her in his arms and dance with her all night. The Captain's Banquet was tomorrow, and they always held a dance afterward. If he played it right, he might get his wish. Maybe he couldn't have all the dances, but he'd try hard for at least one.

"Are you sorry you missed the trip to Salamanca?" he asked.

She cocked her head. "I thought of going, but between Dad and Grandfather and you, the paranoia about my safety is too much and I'd rather not deal with it."

"I'm sorry I couldn't go ashore today. The trip to Salamanca is over a hundred and twenty kilometers, I couldn't be away from the ship for such a long time." He'd been putting out fires instead. A long day of keeping up with more problems than they usually had aboard.

She took a step closer and rested her arms on the top railing. "You're fine, don't apologize. It felt good to have a slower day to catch up with everything and everyone."

"Did you talk to your father then?"

She grimaced. "I did. The mandatory proof that I haven't been kidnapped." She turned sideways and looked at him. "And you, what kept you busy all day?"

Matias reined in another grin at the way they were sharing the little mundane details of their lives with each other while they'd been apart. "We had a large share of minor problems."

"Nothing too serious, I hope."

"No, mostly inconvenient and annoying." He shrugged.

"Those are some strong words," she said with a smile. "What could have been annoying that you're still thinking about it now?"

"The case of the missing pants, for one," he said.

Vanessa chuckled, then covered her mouth. "I'm sorry, but that's too funny. Who's the poor person who's going around without pants?"

"That would be me, and no, I'm not going around without pants, as you can well see." He stepped back and gestured at himself.

Vanessa gave him a long once-over and then quickly looked elsewhere when she caught him watching her.

He couldn't resist the chance to tease her. "Were you checking me out, Vanessa?"

She brought her hands to her cheeks. "No, I'm not checking you out. I'm just looking at your pants. Why are they missing?"

If he'd had enough light to see better, he'd most likely find her blushing.

"Nobody knows. I'm down to only this pair," he said. "Sometimes I send uniform pants and shirts ashore to the nearest hotel's laundry service. This time I didn't send any, and they went missing anyways. And the extra pair I keep in my closet has a busted seam." Something else that had gone wrong on this trip.

Vanessa cocked her head. "Where is the busted seam? And how much of it is busted?"

Maybe he shouldn't have brought it up. "The material is intact, but the thread is gone in several places like it was pulled out." He waved a hand. "I'm not a sewing expert, so I can't really say what happened."

"And where exactly is this seam? On the inside or outside of the pant leg?"

"It's fine, Vanessa. Don't worry about it. I'm sure the rest of the pants will show up." Hopefully he could wear his dress uniform tomorrow for the formal dinner, but he still needed his everyday uniform pants for the rest of the trip.

"I'm pretty sure I can help, Matias," she said. "You may not be a sewing expert but I know a bit about sewing."

He looked back to her. "You can sew?"

She nodded. "I can sew, I can cook, and I can do flower arrangements. Not to an expert level, but I can get by. Thanks to my dad who wanted me to have all the feminine skills even if I didn't have a mother to raise me."

She leaned forward and tapped him on the arm. "Come on, let me see your pants."

Matias chuckled. "Good thing there's no one else around. What would they say if they heard you asking for my pants?"

"I don't know what you're talking about." She frowned, a little smile at the corner of her lips indicating her teasing tone. "It's just another ordinary day aboard the *Princess Catarina*."

There was nothing ordinary. Not about this trip and not about Vanessa.

Matias brought Vanessa to the fitness room in the lower deck where the light was bright and there was no one else around at that time of night. After retrieving his uniform pants from his cabin, he located a small sewing kit in the sundries room for her to work with.

Vanessa finished up the last stitch, knotted the remaining black thread, and snipped it. She turned the pants inside out and gave them a good shake. "There, all done. It's not a perfect job but most people won't be able to see the difference." She paused, then covered a grin behind her fingers. "Unless they're looking right at your—"

Matias held a hand up. "Yes, I know. Let's not mention it again." Of all the places to have a busted seam, the seat of his pants was not the most convenient one.

She held the pants by the belt loops and inspected the stitches she'd done. "I think the new seam will hold up until you can get it done by a professional with a sewing machine." She handed them over to Matias.

He held the pants as she did. "It looks perfect to me. Thank you."

She nodded. "By the way, you're right about the thread being pulled."

Matias neatly folded the pants in half and draped them over the nearest chair. "What do you mean?"

"I mean it was done on purpose. Someone took a seam ripper and cut the stitches every few inches along the seam."

He frowned. "That doesn't make any sense. Why would somebody do that?"

She paused for a moment. "You might have to ask yourself if there's anyone on board with an interest in humiliating you. And how did they gain access to your uniforms?"

"I usually send my uniforms to the laundry room on this deck, but one of the problems we had last night was a broken washing machine. The linens and passengers take precedence, and the crew knows that." He frowned. "But why? What could they gain from it?"

"I don't know. From what I've seen, your passengers love you and your crew respects and likes you."

"Well, some of the crew might not like me as much as others, but it comes with the position." Being liked by all his crew members wasn't a reasonable expectation. He'd learned that quickly with his first ship and crew.

Vanessa went on. "What's the worst thing that could happen if you don't have any more pants to wear?"

"This is ludicrous." Matias shook his head. "Sure, it would be humiliating to be caught with my pants splitting up in front of the passengers, but other than delay the trip, I don't see how someone could benefit from making my uniform pants disappear."

He stood for a moment and walked to the end of the room and back. Moving around always helped him think better.

Vanessa busied herself putting the needle back inside the sewing kit and rolling the black thread onto the spool, as if giving him time to sort through what they had just discussed. She tucked the small scissors inside the box and closed the lid. Matias watched her, his mind going through all the possibilities. Why would anyone want to delay the trip?

Even if it didn't make any sense, he couldn't put aside the coincidence of so many difficulties on this trip. The ship had failsafe protocols, and the crew ran tests and procedures frequently with the end goal of avoiding or dealing swiftly with any kind of problems, so this was unprecedented.

Vanessa stood from the bench against the wall. "I better return to my cabin."

"I'm sorry to keep you waiting. I got distracted." He grabbed his pants from the back of the chair and walked to the door. "I really appreciate you sewing my pants, Vanessa." She'd come to his rescue once again.

"You're welcome. We wouldn't want to embarrass you in front of the passengers," she added in a teasing voice.

Matias opened the door to the hallway. "I'm not so sure about that. Your tone suggests you'd like to see me split my pants in public."

At his words, she didn't try to hide her amusement. "You have to admit it would be funny to watch."

"Depends on who watched it." He looked squarely at her with a raised eyebrow.

CHAPTER ELEVEN

*V*anessa stepped onto the sun deck just as the first rays of sun peeked over the farthest hill. Now that the ship was on its return trip to Porto, its right side, instead of its left, was docked at the small port. She walked to the prow and stood there. The view was reversed from what she'd gotten used to at the beginning of the trip, and even though they stopped at the same towns, the changes offered a different perspective.

Her own perception had changed in the few short days since she'd boarded. In a way, Grandfather was right, as hard as that was for her to admit, even to herself. How could she have thought to remain unchanged after traveling on these waters, after witnessing the people on the terraced lands and their way of life?

Giving in had not been in her plan. Neither was falling in love with her Portuguese heritage and the cruises on the River Douro. But it wasn't too late to walk away, walk away and pretend her stubborn heart hadn't been softened in the company of a river cruise captain. How could she find the strength to resist him when he was as easily excited from the deck of his ship as one of his first-time passengers was?

She turned at the sound of firm steps behind her.

"Are we meeting for another sunrise?" Matias said as he approached.

"I won't have many more chances aboard." The trip would come to a close in two more days. Watching sunrises from somewhere else would never be the same.

"Admit it, time flies when you're having fun." Matias stopped a few feet away from her.

His hands hovered over the railing, then he slipped them in his pockets as he did more and more of late. Was it something she'd said? He'd been putting more distance between them, as if he couldn't bear to be near her.

Vanessa took a quick breath and wiped her sweaty palms against the side of her jeans. If she didn't ask him now, she'd be left wondering about his behavior. She stepped up to him, and Matias moved back.

"What's going on, Matias?"

He frowned. "What do you mean?"

When she moved closer, he drew his hands out of his pockets.

"You're trying to keep your distance from me." She held her position, her eyes locked on his. "You almost flinched just now when I got closer to you. I noticed it last night too." She swallowed past the lump in her throat. "Did I do something you don't like?"

"I'm keeping my distance from you?" He repeated it as a question, his eyes growing darker and wider, as if trying to understand it himself.

For a long moment, he only gazed at her, wordless and unmoving.

Then something passed in his expression: a determination and transparency of emotion that left her wondering.

Was that attraction she saw in his eyes? No, it couldn't be.

"Maybe—" His voice pitched lower and he cleared his throat. "If I weren't under certain obligations and responsibilities, I'd close some of that distance."

Her heart pounded in her chest and her lips parted, her mouth dry and thick. More than his words, the intensity of his gaze burned through her, and the skin on her arms broke into gooseflesh. Her whole body was attuned to him, the warmth between them, and his scent mingled with the breeze from the river.

Vanessa's ability to articulate any words fled her, and her good sense teetered on the edge of temporary insanity. What if she leaned toward him just now? What if she had the courage to find out what would come of a kiss between them?

When a bird squawked overhead, Matias turned to watch it fly to shore. Vanessa took a deep breath and leaned back against the railing, arms crossed on her chest. She shivered at the letdown of the moment with Matias.

"I had thought of having breakfast here with you, but I don't even have time for a cup of coffee," Matias said. "I'm sorry."

"I'll have breakfast with Agnes Grantham and her friends." She kept her eyes on the river, unable to face Matias.

He turned to leave but then stopped. "Vanessa, slight change of plans for today. I'm sending you ashore with Miguel."

"Why? What's there to do?" She'd forgotten to check the itinerary for today.

"We're leaving after breakfast to the next port, and there's a short visit to a wine-producing farm followed by a wine tasting."

One of these days Vanessa would tell everyone how much she disliked the wine tastings. "I can stay aboard."

"I think you'll like the farm. And I trust Miguel," he added. "You'll be in good hands."

Someone else's hands, not Matias's. "What's going on this evening that's keeping you so busy?"

He shuffled a foot on the deck and a small smile curved his lips. "Well, there is a Captain's Banquet scheduled for tonight, and I am the captain."

"Ah, the fancy dinner sponsored by the captain."

She'd heard some of the other passengers talk about it.

"Don't forget about the dance after the fancy dinner," Matias said over his shoulder as he left around the bridge.

A dance.

Vanessa placed a hand over her stomach, as if it could settle the nerves. Excitement and dread sat on a very fine line today.

"Don't let the banquet intimidate you," a man's voice said from the other side.

Vanessa turned to find Miguel approaching her. She dropped her hands to her side. "I wasn't. I mean, I'm not intimidated." She lied, but more to herself than Miguel.

He smiled lightly. "Good. I hope you'll get on the dance floor."

"Does the captain dance?"

"He does and he likes it too." Miguel leaned forward and crossed his arms on the railing. "Captain Romano is more involved with the social activities than he tries to make it look."

"That fits with what I've learned about him in the past few days." Matias was hard to read at times, and his past was still a mystery to her. "What does he do when he's not on trips?"

Miguel raised an eyebrow and Vanessa quickly corrected herself. "I'm sorry. I shouldn't be asking personal questions about the captain."

"I don't think that's a personal question." He shrugged. "We all know Matias has a large family in

Porto, and he's very dedicated to them. He doesn't have any siblings but lots of cousins, aunts and uncles, and both sets of grandparents." He chuckled. "I've met some of them and they're a crazy bunch. In a good way," he added. "As for personal relationships—"

Vanessa shook her head. "I wasn't going to ask that." She was curious, and she had thought about it, but asking directly about his past girlfriends wasn't the same as knowing how big his family was.

"I can tell you my opinion." He paused as if to think about his words. "From what I've learned working with him in these past few years, Matias is dedicated to his job, and he's very loyal to his family. I know when he finally meets the right person, he'll give the same dedication and loyalty to the woman he loves."

He would. Somehow, she knew that.

Vanessa hesitated at the entrance and peered in to the dining room. Sounds of piano keys and laughing voices came from past the bar. She took a deep breath. At breakfast, when Agnes and her friends had found out Vanessa couldn't dance, they'd insisted she take some lessons before the banquet. Vanessa had tried to beg off, but their arguments had been persuasive enough that she'd agreed in the end.

Before she had time to second-guess herself, she went in. Just then, Agnes Grantham waved at her.

"Vanessa, come join us."

Vanessa walked toward them. Agnes and her husband stood near the piano where Ruth Camden played a few chords of something familiar Vanessa couldn't place. Priscilla Smith and her husband, along with Ruth's husband, sat on the upholstered chairs nearby. They all greeted Vanessa warmly, and Vanessa's apprehensions faded back somewhat.

"Is this outfit okay?" Vanessa gestured at herself. She didn't usually wear her floral-print leggings with her highest heels, but Agnes had suggested it.

Agnes came forth and took Vanessa's hands, then led her in a little twirl. "It's perfect. We just need you to wear something that will allow you to see your feet and learn a few basic steps for tonight." She paused, and her expression turned conspiratorial. "What kind of dress will you be wearing?"

"It's a red chiffon with a V-neck and asymmetrical hemline"—her hand went up to the space between her shoulder and her collar bone—"with beading and sequins at the shoulders." It was an extravagant, elegant piece Juliette had deemed indispensable for Vanessa's cruise attire. "My friend helped me pick it out." Her cheeks heated. "She read the description from the catalog to me quite a few times." Juliette had actually recited it often enough for Vanessa to have it memorized.

Agnes and her friends exchanged a meaningful look. She dropped Vanessa's hand and clapped lightly. "That sounds divine. You'll have the perfect silhouette on the dance floor."

"We can't wait to see it," Priscilla said.

"Thank you." Vanessa didn't know how else to respond to their enthusiasm.

Agnes pulled at her husband's arm. "Alan is the best dancer I know." She met his eyes, and they shared a smile. "And I'm not saying that because I'm married to him. He'll lead you through some simple steps, and you'll see it's not very hard."

"Thank you for taking the time to do this. I don't want to inconvenience you."

Alan Grantham stepped forward. "Even if I spent the next year giving you dancing lessons every day, I'd still be indebted to you for saving my Agnes."

Vanessa nodded. She didn't know what to say without calling more attention to herself. She'd only done what she'd been trained to do, but she understood the way he felt.

"I'm not even sure I'll dance tonight," Vanessa said.

The ladies gasped, and Ruth stopped playing the piano. "Why ever not?" Ruth asked, her hands still poised over the keys.

"Of course you will!" Agnes said.

Their strong reactions surprised Vanessa. "I don't know how to dance." If Dad were here, he'd tell her off. He'd placed her in dance lessons at a young age, but she didn't take to them. How many times had she told him she'd never have need for dancing? "And I don't have a partner. Everyone else on this trip has a partner, but I don't." Ironic how a ship full of senior-aged couples was a sore reminder of her single status. Never mind them being old enough to be her grandparents.

"Oh, don't worry about that," said Priscilla. "We don't just dance with our spouses. We dance with everybody, and I'm sure you'll have plenty of dancing partners tonight. Besides," she added, "Captain Romano is an experienced dancer. He'll know how to lead you."

Vanessa's heart jumped. Would Matias really dance with her? "But I don't know how to follow."

"Alan will teach you the basics," said Agnes. "That's all you need when your partner knows what he's doing."

Arguing with these ladies was most likely useless, but Vanessa's confidence faltered. "I'm sure Captain Romano will have better things to do than dance with me."

"Only if he's lost his good sense. We've all seen the way he looks at you." Agnes winked at Vanessa, her friends nodding in agreement with knowing smiles.

In what way did he look at her? Before Vanessa had time to respond to Agnes' comment, Mr. Grantham took her hands and positioned them for a couple's dance. Ruth Camden resumed playing, and the Smiths stood to dance as well.

"Most dancing tunes are set to a quarter beat." While Agnes Grantham explained, her husband led Vanessa through a set of simple steps. "One, two, three, four," Agnes counted to the rhythm.

Vanessa counted along in her mind, trying to pay attention to Mr. Grantham's feet and her own.

After a few minutes of fumbling and tripping several times, Vanessa stepped away from Mr. Grantham. "I'm sorry. I need a little break." It was useless. How was she going to learn to dance well enough by tonight?

Mr. Grantham took his wife by the hand to the middle of the marble floor. As Ruth played a sweeping melody, the Granthams danced with the agility and elegant movements of a couple who knew each other well. Soon, the Smiths joined in.

Vanessa watched in awe of their graceful turns. "Wow. I'll never be able to dance like that."

Agnes chuckled, not missing a step in her husband's arms. "You're right. Not by tonight you won't." They turned once more. "We weren't very great when we started out."

The possibility of being in Matias's arms passed through her mind again. As long as she kept to uncomplicated steps, maybe she could dance with Matias without it being a complete disaster.

Her phone beeped three times, and Vanessa ignored it.

"Are you going to take that?" Agnes stopped dancing and joined Vanessa.

Vanessa shrugged. "It's probably my dad. I can take it later."

Agnes's expression furrowed a little. "Is everything alright?"

"He's just having a hard time with me being on this trip."

"He's probably worried about you." Agnes patted Vanessa's hand. "That's what father's do."

Dad worried about her the way he had when she was fifteen. But she was an adult now.

Vanessa returned to the dance lessons with Alan Grantham, and she tried to do her best for the next thirty minutes.

After the men left, Agnes called for a tea tray, and it arrived a few minutes later.

"How did you and your husband meet?" Vanessa asked.

"We met at a community dance, if you can believe that. We both came with different people, but we noticed each other right away. I discovered later that he tried to find out who I was. I lived in the neighboring town, and it took me a month to return to that dance hall, but I couldn't get him out of my mind. He'd been there every week at the same time, hoping to see me again. The next time, we came by ourselves. And we danced and we talked all night until very early the next morning." Her expression softened, and she got a faraway look in her eyes. "We went out a few times, but it was more of a formality for the sake of our families. We already knew."

Vanessa stopped, cup in midair. "You knew? You saw each other once, maybe twice, and you knew?" She didn't even try to disguise her shock.

Agnes took a bite of her toast. "We did. We would have gotten married the next week, but my parents would have reacted to that very badly, so Alan and I dated for another two months." She shook her head. "I don't recommend long engagements. It tested our fortitude."

"How could you have known, Agnes?" Vanessa frowned. "It's impossible to find love in nothing more than a couple of coincidences."

"Maybe it is, but we did." Agnes placed her teacup on the saucer. "When you know, you know, and there's no argument about it."

"But how can you learn what's important about the other person? Did it even cross your minds?"

"Not at the time. Like I said, we just knew we were supposed to be together, and the rest didn't seem very important." Agnes shrugged. "Haven't you heard of love at first sight?

Vanessa set her spoon down on the side of the plate. "It's just some myth invented by Hollywood to sell movies. How can you fall in love with someone the first time you see them?"

"It's not about the looks, Vanessa. It's about the connection, here and here." Agnes touched her chest over her heart and then her temple. "And sometimes, all you need is a moment of absolute clear lucidity, a connection so strong you can't pretend it doesn't exist." She paused to take a deep breath. "That's what happened between Alan and me."

Vanessa picked up her teacup and sipped, unwilling to argue with Agnes, who had the authority born from experience. There was no disputing that.

How would it feel to have such a moment of perfect connection with a person who felt the same way?

CHAPTER TWELVE

$\mathcal{M}$atias pushed the door to the galley. Chef Teresa lifted her head from stirring a large bowl at the counter. He'd received a message to come see her as soon as possible, and it didn't sound like good news.

"Captain, I don't know what to tell you," she said, her grip tight on the wooden spoon.

"Don't say that, Chef. I know you can pull it off." Was he trying to convince her or himself?

She turned to one of her assistants and gave her some quick instructions. "That problem we had with the refrigerator on the first day of the trip—I did get that fixed." She put the spoon down and looked at him, daring him to contradict her. He knew better than that.

"So what happened this time?"

"It's been working just the way it's supposed to, and you know just as well as I do that these appliances are practically new."

139

He did know. The ship was only three years old, and it was well maintained between trips. Senhor Valadares didn't skimp on materials or upkeep.

Chef Teresa went on for a few more minutes about the working condition of her kitchen and how well she and her staff took care of everything. Her flushed cheeks and clipped tone added to her words. By now, she'd worked herself up to righteous indignation, and Matias let her talk.

"Chef," Matias said at the first chance. "Please tell me what happened."

"I'll tell you what happened, Captain." She took a breath. "Sabotage," she added after a pause, nodding for emphasis.

Matias stared at her, unable to come up with an appropriate reply. "Sabotage?" he finally repeated.

"How do you explain a state-of-the-art refrigerator unplugged overnight? It didn't unplug itself, I can tell you that."

"No, of course not." Matias crossed an arm and rubbed his chin with his hand.

Could she be right? Was there someone aboard creating accidents and unlucky mishaps with the goal of sabotaging the ship? With what purpose? Whatever it was, it needed to be investigated.

"How can I help, Chef Teresa?"

She blew out a breath. "I need more hands and ingredients. The preparations for dessert were lost, and I have to start over."

He pulled out his smartphone and opened the note application. Within a few minutes, they listed everything she needed and made a plan to see it done. After leaving the galley, Matias called Pedro and divided the list into tasks. He'd have to increase the cruising speed forward after breakfast and then again after lunch, pushing their arrival a whole hour ahead of the usual schedule. Hopefully that would be enough to get everything done.

By early evening, Matias stood at the door to the dining room and looked around. The tables were set with the formal china—the one with the captain's logo and the company's colors. This was the dinner where they went all out: where the presentation, the menu, and the wine selection rivaled that of a three-star Michelin restaurant. Nothing was left to chance and no detail was too small to overlook. Everything looked in place and ready for the Captain's Banquet.

Few people knew of the problems that he and some of the crew had worked to fix since early morning. All they could see was the perfection before their eyes, just as he and the crew had planned.

They'd pulled it off. They always did, only this time it had been harder to accomplish.

Miguel stood to his right, followed by Miss Rialto and Justino, the maître d'. They greeted each couple as they entered the room, and waiters were on hand to escort the passengers to their preassigned tables. Afonso sat at the baby grand in the corner playing background music that filled the air with elegance, and after dessert was served, he'd be lending the tunes for romantic dancing and tender moments. The plan was in motion.

This was the kind of night that made Matias proud of his crew, proud of the ship he commanded, and the job that gave him a career he loved.

So why did his stomach churn each time someone approached the receiving line? More than half the passengers were seated already but Vanessa hadn't come through yet.

When he looked up again, there she was, in line behind Monsieur and Madame Joubert. He rushed through the greetings with the French couple, more anxious to finally have Vanessa enter the dining room than he'd thought possible.

"Good evening, Miss Clark." He smiled wide, unable to hold back the feeling of excitement. How appropriate would it be to offer a compliment on how beautiful she was? As if he could say anything that adequately expressed the way she looked tonight.

The corners of her mouth pulled in a smile. "Good evening, Captain Romano."

When the young waiter approached to escort Vanessa to the table, Matias sent him a curt nod and extended his arm to Vanessa. She looped hers through the crook of his elbow, and Matias squelched a sigh of contentment.

All eyes turned to them as they walked side by side, but he didn't care. She looked exquisite tonight. Her soft blonde hair fell in waves behind her back and the red dress she wore fit as if made for a princess, the long flounces flowing behind her with each step she took and the fitted top hugging her shoulders and all her curves in the most flattering way.

He seated her to the left of his chair. Her scent wafted to him and Matias caught himself from leaning down better soak it in. "I'll be back soon."

How fast could he get through the rest of the receiving line?

Vanessa set the fork down on the edge of the dessert plate. Calling that piece of culinary perfection dessert didn't do it justice. It was a heavenly morsel, the flavor of which she'd imprinted in her memory without even knowing what it was called.

Matias sat to her right, still eating his entrée and talking to a Dutch gentleman. Everyone at the table had shared introductions, as the passengers usually did every evening at dinner, but she'd forgotten the man's name already.

As fancy as the previous dinners had been, the Captain's Banquet was the most elegant affair of the whole trip so far. By now, Vanessa had learned not to be intimidated. She'd looked up a few table etiquette lessons on Youtube, building her level of comfort to a manageable one. She'd even worn a formal evening gown, something she'd never before done in her life. Senior prom wasn't formal enough to count—not compared to this banquet. The dress she wore tonight was the kind that turned heads, something she wasn't used to either. Odd how yards and yards of soft, drapey fabric could lend her the confidence to hold her head high and the courage to consider things she wasn't bold enough to try on a normal day back in Kansas.

How nervous she had been on her first night aboard. It was only a few nights ago, but it felt so much longer. She'd made friends since then and it didn't matter that some of them were old enough to be her grandparents.

But the most unexpected friendship was the one with the captain.

The uniform he wore tonight was different from his usual attire, all shiny brass buttons and shirt-sleeves with cuff links. An elegant black bow tie at his neck lent him an air of refined style.

Matias leaned in her direction and lowered his voice. "I'm sorry I've been so busy tonight. How did the excursion go today?"

"It was nice but not quite the same," she replied in an even tone. It had been a short trip, or she would have said no to going ashore. There was more she wanted to say but it wasn't the right time.

He held her gaze for a moment, his eyes conveying the understanding he didn't speak. Vanessa broke the eye contact first, reaching for her glass of sparkling water. Goodness, she was overreaching, seeing things that weren't there.

The passengers at Vanessa's table started clapping, and everyone in the room turned to look at Matias. Vanessa joined in. She'd been so distracted thinking about him, she'd missed the introduction by Miss Rialto.

Matias excused himself and walked across the room to where the microphone stood.

"Good evening, ladies and gentlemen. I hope you've been enjoying the magnificent dinner that Chef Teresa and her assistants have prepared for us tonight." He gestured to the side where an older woman and two younger ones stood in their kitchen uniforms and toques. The whole room erupted in polite clapping, and they nodded back in acknowledgment. "Tonight's menu and wine carte were selected by me—" he paused for a moment—"under Chef Teresa's careful supervision." A smile softened his expression as the passengers chuckled. "Believe me, you don't want me in charge of dinner." More chuckles. "While you're finishing your desserts and espressos, we'll open the dance floor with Afonso Cortez at the piano." He gestured with his arm and the pianist bowed to light applause. "As is tradition with Gold River Cruises, we'll open the dance with the longest-married couple aboard: Mr. and Mrs. Smith from England, who recently celebrated their sixty-third anniversary." The Smiths waved then rose from their seats and walked to the center of the marble floor.

After a few minutes, Matias walked over to Miss Rialto and led her by the hand to the center of the room.

They danced beautifully, the captain and the cruise director, synchronized and in tune with the music and each other as if they'd been doing it for years. Miss Rialto had the grace of a ballroom dancer in a long black dress, and Matias cut a dashing figure in his dress uniform. They looked perfect together.

Vanessa twisted the napkin on her lap between her fingers. Her neck warmed and something hard knotted her stomach. Maybe she could leave and feign a sudden sickness. It wouldn't be a complete lie; she wasn't feeling well. Even if she spent the rest of the evening in her cabin, it would be better than sitting and watching Matias dance with another woman who had an expression of complete bliss on her face.

Other couples joined the dance floor, and Matias and Miss Rialto traded dance partners with more passengers doing the same. When Vanessa looked around her table, she found it empty. The other couples had already joined the dance, while others sat down at the nearby tables again.

Vanessa placed the napkin on the table by her plate, then scooted her chair back closer to the shadowed wall. As she prepared to stand and leave, the Granthams returned.

Agnes took the neighboring chair. "Why aren't you dancing?"

146

Vanessa shrugged. "I can't dance." She couldn't even pretend.

Alan Grantham stood in front of her and extended his hand. Vanessa didn't take it.

He took her fingers in his and tugged gently. "Come on, young lady. You won't be sitting this one out."

Agnes waved her hand in their direction. "You heard him. Go."

Why had she bought a red dress? It screamed for attention, and that was the last thing she wanted right now. Vanessa walked beside Alan Grantham, reluctant to show her non-existent dance skills in front of the crew and passengers. They danced for a few minutes, and the instruction he'd give her earlier in the day came back to memory. Maybe she could fake it for a little while.

She didn't have the time to get used to dancing with Mr. Grantham. A French gentleman cut in, and Vanessa danced with him for a few minutes, his dancing skills less sharp than Mr. Grantham's. She spied the exit on the other side of the room, farther than what she needed at the moment.

"May I cut in?" Matias's smooth voice sounded at her shoulder.

Before Vanessa could respond, she found herself expertly and swiftly transferred from the French man's arms to Matias's. His hand settled on her back, the other firmly cradling her hand and, as the music changed to a slower measure, Matias adjusted his pace to her faltering one.

"Miss Clark," he said to her, a smile tinting his voice. "Are you enjoying yourself tonight?"

What could she say, with so many other couples around them, several of them openly staring at her and Matias?

"Yes, I am, Captain Romano," she replied with a pleasant expression and a neutral smile, ordering her galloping heart to calm down and not betray her.

How could she want to leave and long to stay at the same time? It was maddening.

The physical proximity between them muddled her senses. She couldn't think straight. His scent, his solid biceps beneath her hand, the warmth of his body against hers. Was this what dancing did to people? Every point of contact between her and Matias rushed her into hyper-sensitivity.

He leaned in. "This is not the way I wanted to dance with you."

Vanessa hid a grimace. "I'm sorry. I know I can't dance, not like Miss Rialto danced with you." That sounded pettier than she'd meant.

Matias arched an eyebrow and looked at her. He opened his mouth as if to say something, then closed it again. His pace quickened and he led them into a wide turn, to the periphery of the dance floor, Vanessa struggling to keep up with him. Once there, he slowed again.

"It's part of the protocol for the captain and the cruise director to follow the first dance." His calm voice was matter-of-fact, as if reciting from the book of rules. "Miss Rialto has had dance training as part of her job."

Maybe it was the protocol, but Miss Rialto had enjoyed it too much.

After another turn, Matias leaned in. "What I meant to say was that I wanted to dance with you without the other passengers around."

Vanessa stopped and her eyes widened, unable to look away from Matias. She dropped her arms to the side and took a step back from him.

"We'll have a ten-minute break," the pianist said on the microphone. He brought the melody to a close, and the passengers clapped politely.

Matias joined the clapping for a moment. He stepped closer to her and guided her back to the table with a hand on her lower back, the warmth from his fingers radiating through the thin fabric sending a pleasant tingle up her spine.

"Thanks for the dance, Miss Clark." He pulled out the chair for her and as Vanessa sat down, he bent and whispered in her ear. "Meet me at the bridge in one hour?"

Vanessa turned to look up at him, his eyes matching his tone, half hope and half uncertainty. So much like her own feelings.

An elderly passenger approached Matias and asked him a question. As the two walked away from the table, Matias looked over his shoulder at Vanessa. Before she had the presence of mind to nod back at him, another passenger took Matias's attention.

Yes, she would meet him at the bridge. How could she not?

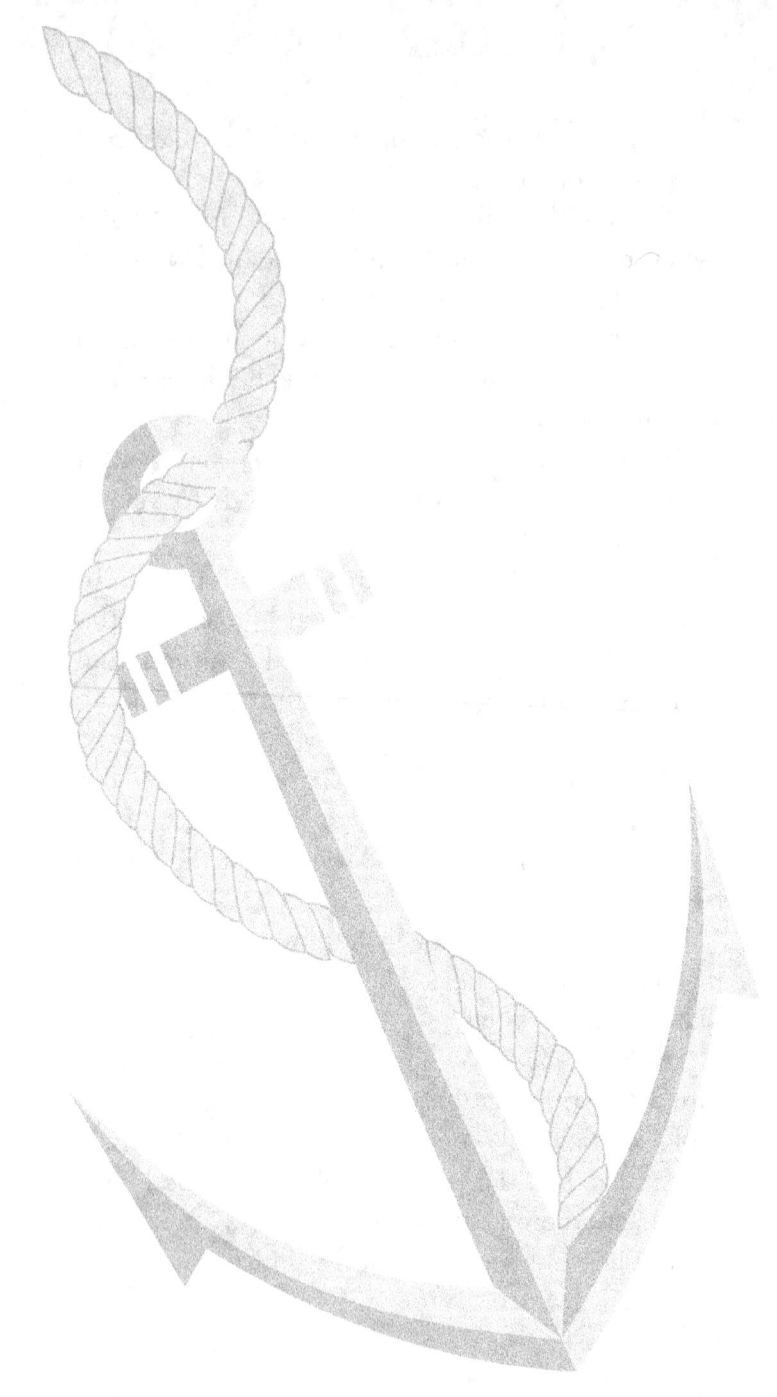

CHAPTER THIRTEEN

$\mathcal{M}$atias hurried up the steps to the sun deck. Was Vanessa waiting for him at the prow behind the bridge?

He'd told her one hour, but he was late. He usually mingled with the passengers during the dance and afterward, and on some trips even ended up in the bar with a few of them after hours.

But tonight, when he actually wanted to leave the dance, he'd had to split his attention between passengers and problems on the lower deck.

The sun deck was empty. Not many passengers had the fortitude to climb the ladder after an evening of good eating and liberal drinking.

Matias sprinted the last few meters toward the bridge. He and Miguel had pulled down the blinds and locked the small room. They'd return in the early morning for the fail-safe procedures before departure.

As he rounded the bridge past the window, his hope fell. Vanessa wasn't there. Had she come at all, or had he missed her?

He leaned against the railing and his head dropped. He couldn't catch a break. Not on this ill-fated trip.

"You're late, Captain."

Matias whirled around at the sound of her voice. "Vanessa." He straightened, and his smile grew wider. "You came."

She stepped forward from the shadow on the other side of the bridge and held up her fingers in a little wave. "I came."

She lifted the hem of her dress. "Do you know how hard it is to climb up to the sun deck with these shoes?"

He walked to her. "I was counting on that." He lifted a finger in front of his lips and lowered his voice. "Shh. Don't tell anyone." At her puzzled expression, he explained. "From experience, I know that not many passengers come up here after the banquet. But, just in case, I'll help you on the way down so you don't fall." Another accident was the last thing he needed.

Her expression softened, and the corner of her mouth lifted. "Watch what you say, Captain. That sounds premeditated."

Of course he'd planned to see her alone. If that was premeditation, then he'd confess to it. "Guilty."

That elicited another smile from her. "Since you're confessing, are you going to tell me why you asked me to meet you here?"

Matias bridged the distance between them until they stood in front of each other. "I really wanted to dance with you." The breeze blew stray hairs in front of her, and Matias brushed them off, his fingers skimming across her shoulder.

"And the music?"

"In my pocket." He reached into his coat pocket and withdrew his smartphone. With a few taps, Matias brought up the playlist he'd compiled earlier. He swiped the volume on high and propped the phone on the floor against the bridge's outside wall. It was loud enough for them to hear it, but not so loud as to draw attention.

Then he turned up his palm toward her. "May I have this dance, Vanessa?"

She placed her hand in his. "As long as you don't mind being stepped on."

Matias brought her closer to him. "I don't mind." Not one little bit.

Vanessa took a breath, releasing it slowly, and he found himself doing the same. Was she as nervous as he was?

In her heels, their bodies fit comfortably at the same height, hip to hip, chest to chest. He gripped her fingers and pressed his cheek against hers. She smelled of ripe fruit and bright sun, like a summer day in the countryside. He inhaled, committing the scent to memory, willing his mind to remember the softness of her skin, the hushed brushing of her dress against his pants, the way his heart skipped in time with the beating of her pulse under his thumb. The sounds of the summer night and the flowing river mingled with the ballads playing on his phone and, for this moment alone, nothing else mattered.

"I've been meaning to tell you how amazing you look in that dress," he said in a low voice.

Her pacing faltered for a moment, but she quickly recovered. "Thank you. Juliette forced me to buy it."

"Who's Juliette?"

"My roommate from college."

"Please send my heartfelt thanks to Juliette. She has extremely good taste."

Her expression bloomed into a smile. "You like it that much?"

"Only because you're wearing it."

As the music played on, she relaxed, and they grew more comfortable with each other. They stood together, shuffling more than dancing and not really paying attention to the tempo in each song. But he didn't care. He had her in his arms, and that was all that mattered.

"This is nice," he said. It was a lot more than nice, but even if he'd known any poetry to recite by heart, the words would have failed him. "If I had the magic to make a moment last forever, this would be it."

Vanessa pulled back a little to look him in the eyes. "This very moment?"

He stopped and met her gaze. In the waning moonlight and the floodlights of the ship, her eyes had a subdued sparkle. But the question was there, and he replied to it the only way he knew how.

With a hand around her back and the other on the side of her face, Matias leaned in and brushed his lips against hers. Vanessa didn't pull back. She grabbed on to his upper arms instead. When she parted her mouth in a soft sigh, Matias deepened the kiss.

This. This was the moment he wanted to keep.

Vanessa was dreaming. She was in a beautiful dream, and she didn't want to wake up.

Matias kissed her softly at first, as if giving her time to withdraw. She didn't, and the kiss became more insistent, more urgent, eased only by a row of short little kisses, allowing her to catch her breath in between each one before going back for seconds. He tasted of chocolate and coffee and the Portuguese dessert wine they'd served after dinner, and she wanted all the seconds she could have.

More and more and more.

Her head spun and her blood rushed as she wrapped her arms behind his neck to ground herself. Her shoes slipped, and Matias brought her up against him, erasing the last inch between them. He groaned in a short exhale, and Vanessa sighed, parting her lips, and when he deepened the kiss for the briefest of seconds, her knees buckled and she slipped from his grasp.

Matias stood firm and held on to her, or she would have surely fallen. Her cheeks flamed and her chest heaved. Was it the lack of air or the heat inside her that was making it hard to breathe? She closed her eyes, unsure of what feelings coursed through her.

She remained in his arms for a while longer, her pulse slowing and the heat cooling. Matias kept a hand on her back, stroking gently in small circles. He placed a soft kiss on her forehead and stepped back, his hands lingering from her forearms down to her hands in a long caress, until nothing else connected her to him but the tips of their fingers.

Vanessa opened her eyes, grateful for the semidarkness in which to hide her emotions. Because if someone shone a bright light on them right now, Matias would see everything on her face.

"Vanessa." His voice came out scratchy, and he cleared his throat. "I guess now we know which moment to keep."

To keep and to hold forever. A moment to never forget.

She'd been kissed before. She'd even thought she'd had strong feelings for those other guys who'd kissed her. But the connection she felt to Matias went beyond any reasonable explanation she could give herself— a chemistry of the soul, the heart, the body. Never mind they'd known each other only since Monday. He'd turned her world upside down in merely six days.

She bent down and adjusted her shoes, then turned to the river where the darkness was a welcome refuge. What could she say to Matias that wouldn't make her sound crazy?

He stopped at her side and took her hand in his. His sleeve brushed against her arm, and Vanessa glanced down at their entwined fingers. When she looked back up at him, he brought her hand to his lips and kissed it.

"Matias," she started, all the words swirling in her head and none making it to her mouth.

A series of insistent beeps interrupted her from the floor and they both turned their attention to it. Matias retrieved his phone from where he'd propped it when they were dancing.

He swiped at the screen, and its light showed Matias's features for a moment, his eyebrows scrunched in a frown. "I'm sorry. I need to take this."

He didn't walk away and didn't turn his back. Instead, he reached for her hand and took it again.

Her heart jumped and she brought her free hand to her chest, as if it could calm the racing inside her. That sense of belonging returned to her, strong and undeniable.

Matias answered the phone. "Yes?"

A male voice replied to him. Matias listened and his expression tensed. "Right now? You're sure? In the lounge?" After a short pause he added, "I know."

He let go of her hand and turned off the screen, then slipped the phone in the pocket of his pants. For a moment, he said nothing.

"Do you need to go to the lounge?"

He nodded. "I do, but you need to come with me."

CHAPTER FOURTEEN

*V*anessa took a deep breath when they arrived at the entrance to the dining room. Matias placed a hand on her lower back, and she stepped forward. Past the tables and chairs, the lounge was bathed in soft light. The pianist had left, and ambient music played through the sound system instead. Behind the bar, a man in a white shirt stood sideways to them, shaking a small metal canister in his hands.

Matias had been cryptic, not telling her why she needed to come to the lounge with him. Dread filled the pit of her stomach. It was bad enough they'd left the sun deck without discussing the earth-shattering kiss they'd shared. Maybe it was for the best. She wouldn't have known what to say.

In less than forty eight hours, the ship would dock in Porto and the uncertainty between them would only increase.

Why had she kissed the captain? That was one kiss she'd have a hard time forgetting.

Miguel approached Matias and took him aside. They exchanged a few words and then Miguel left.

"What's going on, Matias?"

He tipped his head toward the bar. "Come on. We'll talk over there."

When they arrived, the barman turned around. "Hello, Vanessa."

She gasped. "Grandfather?"

He poured the contents of the small canister inside a glass, his movements slow and measured.

Matias stepped aside, back straight. "Good evening, sir. Welcome aboard."

Vanessa's jaw went slack. "You knew? You knew he was here, and you didn't tell me?"

Grandfather braced a hand on the bar in her direction. "Don't blame Captain Romano, Vanessa. I wanted to come and I didn't give anyone else much choice."

She shook her head and took a step back. "I can't do this. Not right now."

Grandfather moved from around the bar. "I'm not staying, but I'd like a few minutes. Please."

Vanessa stopped. She'd hid her clenched hands in the folds of her dress. Slowly, she released each finger, easing the tension from her body.

Grandfather reached for the glass and downed the amber liquid in one gulp. "Captain, I will need a word with you before I go."

Matias nodded.

Grandfather hesitated. "Can we step out to the balcony? I promise I'll be brief."

Vanessa folded her arms around her waist and nodded. She followed him to the space just outside the lounge. He left the sliding door partially open and, through the tinted glass, Matias stared at them from a barstool. She moved to the railing, and Grandfather settled a few yards away.

For a man in his mid-sixties, he looked younger. His hair was gray at the temples but it suited him. He wore a pair of black pants and a white shirt with the sleeves rolled up. Nobody would ever guess that behind the simple outfit stood a powerful man.

"I named this ship after your mother. Did you know that?"

"What?" Vanessa turned to him, unable to hide the surprise from her face. "My mother's name was Ana, not Catarina."

His expression softened. "Yes, Ana Catarina. Ana is just a filler name, like Maria. We always called her Catarina." He spoke English fluently with a strong accent.

Vanessa took a deep breath. Why had Dad never told her Mom's full name? Something so simple. Instead she was learning this from a man she didn't really know.

"When I started plans for this ship, I knew I wanted it to be the most elegant river cruise ship in Portugal, so I named it after her because she was my little princess." He paused for a moment and his voice pitched lower. "A father never really outgrows that, you know? Thinking of his only daughter as the princess in his life."

Did Dad think of Vanessa that way too? He sure acted like the king, controlling and interfering, always checking on her.

Grandfather went on. "My next ship will the finest in Europe, and I already have a name for it." He smiled wide and then sobered. "But you're not here to listen to my construction plans. I've been asking Captain Romano to come aboard since the first day, but he repeatedly said no."

"Why did you want to come aboard?" The words slipped her mouth. She didn't want to be curious, but how could she stay indifferent to this man who was related to her? The man who'd raised the woman whom Vanessa never got the chance to know as a mother.

He sighed deeply and rubbed his chin. "Because I wanted to see you on the ship. To see your reaction to everything." His hand went wide. "That's why I came in today when I knew Captain Romano would be busy with the banquet. I contacted the security team directly."

They stood quietly at the railing. Vanessa's mind whirled with the unanswered questions she'd had all her life, but she asked none. Too many emotions battled inside her, and she wasn't ready to sort through any of them. Between a father who had a hard time letting go of her and a grandfather who wanted to be closer, the pressure to live up to their expectations was more than she could take today.

And then there was Matias. Where did he fit in her life?

The rustling of paper brought Vanessa back from her thoughts to the grandfather beside her.

"I won't take more of your time." He extended an envelope in her direction. "But I would like you to read this."

"Right now?" The slight nervousness in her voice slipped through. What was in that envelope?

"Sometime when you're up for it."

She took the envelope, and he thrust his hands in his pockets.

He turned to leave but then paused and stepped forward to place a quick goodbye kiss on her cheek, the way so many Portuguese people did.

"I do hope you'll enjoy the rest of the trip, Vanessa."

She only nodded, unwilling to say anything to him. Not really knowing what to say.

Matias stood when Grandfather approached, and he looked in Vanessa's direction before leaving together. With the tinted window, he wouldn't be able to see her face, but she could see his and the apprehension wrinkled into his forehead.

Vanessa waited a few minutes and then left to her cabin, grateful the hallway was empty at the late hour. Once inside, she locked the door behind her and threw the envelope onto the bedside table. She kicked off her shoes and wrestled with her dress for five minutes before she was able to remove it without damaging the fabric.

After changing into her comfortable clothes and cleaning off her makeup, Vanessa sat on the side of the bed. The envelope lay on the polished wood surface, wrinkled from where she'd grabbed it by the corner. She picked it up again and ran a palm over the front where Grandfather had written her name. If only she could read the words inside that way, without breaking the flap. There would be no turning back.

Before she lost her nerve, Vanessa tore the side and pulled out the page.

Dear Vanessa,

My greatest regret in life is missing out on you growing up. The day I lost my only daughter, I also lost my only granddaughter when your father decided to take you back to the USA. As a father, I understand why he did it. I would have done the same thing. But as a grandfather, I mourned losing my place in your life. When the opportunity came to bring you aboard a cruise trip, I jumped at it. Your mother loved the water, be it ocean or river. She loved being on the ships, learning about them, seeing them work. And I wanted to give you the chance to fall in love with the ship and the river as well.

You remind me so much of her. Your hair is lighter and you have your father's eyes, but you have her nose. You also have her sense of curiosity, her work ethic, and her compassion toward others. Even if I didn't see you grow up, I'm proud of the woman you've become and I know your mother would have been too.

Looking back, I realize that having a family reunion dinner on your first night in Portugal might have not been my best idea. Your grandmother warned me, but I was so excited for you to meet your uncles, aunts, and cousins, I didn't even stop to consider how overwhelming it was for you. I'm sorry for the stress it caused you. Whether you stay or go back, I'll accept your decision. My only hope is this experience will be a fond memory for you one day.

With love,

Your grandfather/António Valadares

Vanessa wiped her cheek with her fingers. The tears had started falling when she read the first paragraph, and they wouldn't stop. She sat back against the headboard and wrapped her arms around her knees. A shuddering breath shook her chest and she breathed in deeply a few times.

This letter was not what she'd expected. She'd spent almost two weeks in Porto before boarding the *Princess Catarina*, and she hadn't taken the time to know Grandfather, Grandmother, or any of her other family members. She'd been dismissive and rude and an all around pain to deal with, hiding in her apartment and ignoring their efforts to connect. No wonder Matias had thought she was a spoiled brat—she'd been one.

This letter bore the words of a man who knew loss. He'd loved deeply and had lost dearly.

Dad had lied to her. He could call it whatever he wanted, but he'd kept from her the precious knowledge she'd craved growing up: the stories about her mother, the existence of caring grandparents and extended family.

She jumped from bed and searched for her phone. When she found it, she dialed Dad's number, but the call wouldn't go through. All the times Dad had called and she hadn't answered. Now she wanted to talk to him and couldn't. So much irony.

Maybe Matias had a phone she could use. She caught sight of her face in the mirror behind the door and started. Definitely not at her best right now. After looking so well put-together this evening, she'd scare Matias with her red, swollen eyes and ratty hair.

In the bathroom, Vanessa splashed some cold water on her splotchy face and combed her hair into a pony tail. It was the best she could do on short notice.

It was about time she got some of the answers she'd always wanted.

Matias accompanied Senhor Valadares to his car parked near the dock. When the driver saw them approaching, he threw a cigarette onto the ground and smashed it with the tip of his shoe.

Matias had left his uniform coat behind and the river breeze was welcome.

Senhor Valadares leaned against the back of the car and crossed his arms. He tipped his chin at the driver, and the driver walked away in the other direction.

"I'm sorry for interrupting your evening, Captain. I know how busy you are, especially on the night of the banquet."

Matias slipped his hands in his pockets. "You're welcome any time. It's your ship, sir. And your grand-daughter," he added.

"Vanessa." Senhor Valadares sighed and shook his head. "She probably won't forgive me for waylaying her like this."

He glanced at Matias, but Matias didn't comment. The situation was delicate enough already without him offering his opinion on the matter. Not that he had any right to do so anyway.

"Speaking of my granddaughter. You and Vanessa seemed close when you arrived at the lounge. Was that only my impression?"

Matias kicked a pebble, buying some time. "Uh, we were dancing on the sun deck." His ears flamed. He and Vanessa had been doing more than just dancing. He wouldn't lie about it if asked directly, but he needed time to think through his feelings for Vanessa. He wanted to talk to her before confessing anything to her grandfather.

Senhor Valadares raised an eyebrow at him. "Dancing? Come see me on Monday, Captain. At the main office in the city."

"Yes, sir." He straightened and made eye contact with his boss. Under the street-light, Senhor Valadares's face stood out against the night's darkness. Vanessa's words came to his mind about her nose and her mother. Her grandfather had a more masculine version of the same nose. Had Vanessa noticed the common family trait she shared with her grandfather?

Senhor Valadares signaled his driver who returned promptly. He opened the back door, and Senhor Valadares paused before entering. "And the excursions? Did she like them?" He turned to Matias, his tone laced with expectant hope.

Matias nodded. "I believe so. She was quite taken with Castelo Rodrigo."

The older man smiled. "That's a good sign. It was her mother's favorite stop on this route."

After the car left, Matias went back to the ship. He stopped at the reception desk to retrieve his coat.

"Matias."

When he looked up, Vanessa stood from the seat across the lobby and practically ran to him.

"Vanessa. I thought you went to your cabin." He glanced at the analog clock on the wall. "It's past two in the morning."

She followed his glance, then turned back to him. "I can't go to sleep until I talk to my Dad, and my phone isn't working."

He touched her shoulder. "Is everything alright?"

"I need to ask him a question." She folded her arms and blinked before meeting his eyes. "Do you have a phone I can use? Please."

"You can use mine." Matias reached in his pocket and unlocked the screen, then handed the phone to her.

She didn't take it. "It's an international call, Matias."

He placed the phone in her hand. "I know. Go and make your call. I'll wait here."

After a moment of hesitation, Vanessa took the phone. "I'll be back in a few minutes."

She clutched the phone to her chest, and he watched her go, her shoulders slumped and her posture heavy. What was going on between her and her father?

Matias removed his bow tie and slipped it into his pocket. He walked to the large glassed wall behind the staircase and watched the dock.

What a night. One he wouldn't easily forget.

He'd gotten his wish and had his private dance with Vanessa. From holding her in his arms to kissing her had only been the natural progression of their attraction and the growing relationship between them. Somewhere in the past few days he'd stopped seeing her as the bratty girl from their first encounter and he found himself craving her company. Her smiling face, her voice, her nearness and touch. There wasn't a part of her Matias didn't want.

He'd even broken his rule to never become involved with a passenger and it would be lying to say he regretted it.

Regret didn't factor in.

For years he'd been avoiding dating and relationships, splitting his time between his family and his career, not really missing what he didn't have in his life and not minding his single status.

But then Vanessa had come along and all of that had completely changed: he wanted a friend, a companion to dance with, to talk and to listen to, a woman he could embrace and kiss until morning came.

Not any woman. Only she would do.

CHAPTER FIFTEEN

*M*atias unlocked the bridge and went in for the morning's procedures. He'd had only a few hours of sleep after the events of the previous night, but his duties aboard didn't wait for him to rest and catch up. He'd do that when he got to his apartment in a few days. For now, work went on as usual, and he still had to navigate the ship to one more port before returning to its home destination.

As tired as he felt, his thoughts turned back to Vanessa.

She hadn't said much after returning his phone, but he could see she'd been crying. If only he could have taken her in his arms and offered the comfort she'd so obviously needed. But one kiss didn't give him the right to barge into her life when so much was still left unsaid between them.

171

The trip was coming to an end. Dinner tonight was the last one aboard—a farewell from the crew to the passengers. By morning, they'd be back to Porto. Passengers would disembark after breakfast, as they always did. He'd be on deck saying goodbye and posing for some last-minute pictures. But how could he go through the rituals when it came to Vanessa's turn on the gangway?

The rest of the morning passed without incident. Matias didn't see Vanessa at breakfast and hopefully that meant she'd slept in. She needed it. She also missed the tour to Lamego, but more than half the passengers usually did as the busyness of the previous days' excursions caught up to them. By lunchtime, Matias was anxious to see her, and he found excuses to linger in the dining room, hoping she'd show up, but she didn't. He returned to the bridge and got the ship on its way to Régua, and Miguel took over from there.

An hour later, when he peeked again in the dining room, Vanessa was there. Everyone was already finished with lunch, and the busboys had cleaned up. The wait staff had started setting up for dinner and she sat in the farthest corner, away from the preparations. He watched her for a moment as she stirred a cup of tea, her shoulders hunched and her movements timid and small.

He shelved his earlier resolve to give her some space and walked over to her table.

"Good afternoon, Miss Clark."

172

Vanessa raised her eyes from the plate, and the corner of her mouth rose in a wan smile. "Captain."

Matias pulled out a chair and sat one chair away from her. "Did you get to rest?"

She pushed away a plate with a half-eaten piece of toast. "I didn't fall asleep until after six in the morning." She leaned an elbow on the table and cupped her chin in her hand. "I grew up with a view of my past that I'm now finding out is not completely true. And I'm not dealing very well with it." After a brief pause she added, "I don't know why I'm unloading all this on you." She sat back and folded her hands on her lap.

Matias pulled his chair closer to her. "I'd like to think of myself as your friend, and friends help friends, even if it's just with a listening ear." He wanted to be more than her friend, but friendship was a good way to start. "What happened last night between—"

She shook her head. "I can't think of what happened last night between us." She looked away to the window for a moment. "Not right now. Is that okay? I know we should want to talk about it, but I have so much going on, and this is not reality." Her arms drew a wide circle around them. "This is not who I am, Matias. The fancy clothes, the elegant dinner, the dancing. None of it feels real. I'm just a simple girl from Kansas. I don't go around changing outfits two or three times a day, and I certainly don't spend my time sipping tea and lounging by the pool. Do

173

you understand what I'm saying?" Her eyes shone with a kind of pleading emotion that compelled him to her.

His hand touched her forearm. "I know this is not your normal." He kept his voice low. "But you have to know that I'm not my job. As much as I love captaining this ship, it's what I do, not who I am. I don't wear this uniform on land. Heck, I dance only when I'm aboard." His voice rose at the last word, and he reined himself in. Was the earnestness in his tone enough to convince her he understood?

She held his gaze. "Can you wait until I'm ready?"

Waiting wasn't the problem. "Will you let me stay in contact with you after the trip?"

His phone beeped and he glanced at the screen. It was a message from Miguel. Matias glanced at Vanessa. "Excuse me. I need to take this."

"Yes, of course," she replied.

When he unlocked the screen, two words glared up at him: COME NOW!

Matias rose and looked out the closest window. Something was wrong. Instead of the usual expanse of river ahead of the bow, the ship leaned toward the left bank. "I have to go."

She stood from the table as he sprinted toward the lobby. When the jolt came, Matias braced himself on the door jamb. Shouts sliced through the air but he didn't stop. He kept running toward the sun deck even as the impact dragged and finally stalled the ship.

In the bridge, blinking lights and alarm sounds assailed the front of the console. Matias grabbed the microphone. "Emergency personnel, assess and report."

Miguel stood at the wheel, facing the prow.

Matias snatched the emergency procedure folder from the shelf and opened it on the counter. "Port Authority?" he asked.

Jaime pointed at Pedro. "On the phone, sir."

Pedro nodded and continued talking to the person on the other side.

Miguel turned off several of the switches on the console. His expression was calm but his movements belied the tension in the bridge.

When he was done, he lifted his eyes to Matias. "We lost the rudder."

Vanessa ran to the sliding doors and stepped outside. Something had happened to the ship. It appeared to be stuck on a sandbar in a perpendicular position to the river, too close to the eastern bank.

The loudspeaker squeaked and Matias's voice came on. "Emergency personnel, assess and report." Despite the curtness of the command, he sounded in control. Her anxiety subsided.

She ran back to the lobby, where several crew members were already assisting passengers. Some people were visibly shaken. Others were less obviously affected, but the nervousness was still evident in their eyes.

"Your attention, please." Matias spoke again. "This is Captain Romano. We are not in danger of sinking. We ask that you remain calm and stay away from the balconies and open decks. Thank you."

For the next fifteen minutes, under Afonso Cortez's direction, she helped treat some minor injuries. One of the French ladies had passed out and now lay recovering on a sofa in the lounge, her husband keeping her company. Little by little, passengers came to the dining room to await more news and speculation abounded. Crew members went around, offering water and trying to keep everyone calm.

Vanessa found the Granthams sitting with their friends and approached them. "How is everyone?"

Agnes laid a hand on her wrist. "We're okay. No injuries. Just a little nervous to see what's going on."

Vanessa nodded. "I'm sure the captain is doing all he can—"

His voice interrupted. "Ladies and gentleman, this is Captain Romano speaking. Due to some unforeseeable circumstances, the ship's rudder has sustained some damage, causing the ship to drift into a sand bank."

Several people around Vanessa gasped, and others started murmuring.

"As I said earlier, we are not in danger of sinking." He paused for a moment, as if to let the information settle. "I repeat, we are not in danger of sinking. That said, we will be following protocol. Another ship, the *Alma Vida*, is on its way and we will be transferring all the passengers directly when it arrives, sometime in the next hour. This ship will take you to Régua, the closest port."

This time the collective murmurs and gasps sounded louder, and other passengers asked for silence.

"In the meantime, Port Authority is already on its way for support and assistance. Several of the staff will be available to answer questions and to offer any assistance you may need in getting ready for the transfer. Once you arrive in Régua, there will be buses to take you to one of the local hotels, and in the morning you'll take the same buses back to Porto." He paused for a breath. "On behalf of Gold River Cruises and the *Princess Catarina*, I apologize for the situation and the inconvenience to you. Upon disembarking, there will be company representatives to assist you in any way. Thank you for your attention and, again, I'm sorry."

Vanessa rose and excused herself. When she arrived at the lobby, Matias was already there, surrounded by crew members and other passengers. He looked at her from across the room and nodded briefly. Talking to him right now was out of the question; she'd have to wait for another opportunity.

A few minutes later, Matias announced that the Port Authority ship had arrived with several smaller boats to close the river traffic in both directions. He urged the passengers to not be alarmed at the loud noise and activity coming from the river around the ship.

The Granthams stopped to talk to her. "Are you getting ready to leave?"

She shook her head. "I'm going to stay and help Afonso with the transfer, just in case."

Agnes raised an eyebrow, and Vanessa hurried on to explain. "Afonso, the pianist. He's also the emergency specialist."

"Oh, yes, I remember his help." Agnes patted her hand. "I'm sure he appreciates your assistance."

Outside, the noise of the smaller boats tapping against the hull of the *Princess Catarina* drew her attention.

Mr. Camden gestured toward the window. "The Port Authority is anchoring a boat against the *Princess Catarina* to prevent further drifting."

"We remember seeing the other ship the captain mentioned, the *Alma Vida*," Alan Grantham said. "It's one of the larger day-cruise ships. A very nice one."

Vanessa raised a hand to her chest as she and the others approached the window. They couldn't see the Port Authority boats from this side, but several police cars and one fire truck had parked along the road by the bank and had closed the access. Some of the locals had come out to watch, as if the event were worthy entertainment.

The Camdens and the Smiths approached Vanessa. "We thought it would be best to say goodbye now, in case we don't have time later," Ruth Camden said.

"Oh. You're right." Vanessa nodded at them. "We might not have the time with everything going on."

Ruth and Priscilla hugged Vanessa, and their husbands shook her hand. Priscilla slipped a piece of paper into Vanessa's hand. "Our contact info, from all of us." She gestured to include the group. "If you ever find yourself in England, come and see us."

Vanessa smiled. "I will. I've always wanted to visit England."

Alan Grantham stepped forward and wrapped his arms around Vanessa's shoulders. "We'll hold you to it, young lady." His voice caught. "You have my gratitude forever."

Vanessa swallowed past the lump in her throat and returned the hug. When Agnes took her in her arms, the tears rolled, despite Vanessa's efforts to hold them in. "Vanessa, I'm so glad we had the chance to get to know you and become friends," Agnes said when she stepped back.

"I am too, Agnes." Vanessa hadn't expected to make friends with the senior passengers.

Agnes tipped her head in Matias's direction. "Remember what I told you about connections."

Vanessa protested but Agnes stopped her. "Just listen with your heart, Vanessa."

When the transfer ship arrived, the Port Authority captain positioned one of his boats along the *Princess*

Catarina and connected the gangway between the two vessels. Anabela Rialto and her assistants had assigned the passengers to boarding groups based on medical needs and age, and other crew members helped organize the line.

Miguel brought up the rear. Miss Rialto stood next to him with a clipboard in her hands and crossed off the names of the passengers before they stepped off.

The next hour went by in a blur activity as the crews cooperated to assist groups of passengers onto the transfer boat, which in turn took them to the *Alma Vida,* everyone working together with a common goal.

Matias had taken the front of the line and personally greeted the passengers by name as he handed them over the gangway, apologizing and thanking them at the same time. For a moment, he made eye contact with Vanessa, his expression guarded. She held his gaze, but when the next passenger approached, Matias gave him his attention.

She didn't want to say goodbye to him. Not like this. Not today.

CHAPTER SIXTEEN

$\mathcal{M}$atias said goodbye to the last passenger and waved as the transfer boat took the group to the *Alma Vida*. It had taken three trips to evacuate all the passengers, and it would take one more for the crew.

Not quite all the passengers.

He walked over to Miss Rialto, who handed him the passenger manifest. "That was not the last passenger, Captain."

He took the clipboard from her and scanned the list. "Thanks, Miss Rialto. Please get the crew ready for transferring. We'll be back in a few minutes."

Miguel followed him down the stairs to the lobby in the upper deck where the passengers' luggage sat in rows.

"Is everything tagged?" Matias asked.

"Yes, and I already gave the list to the crew of the *Alma Vida*." Miguel held the copy. "They'll start moving the luggage after our crew transfers."

Matias slipped his tie off and opened an extra button on his shirt. "Did you talk to everybody?" Including himself and Miguel, there were forty crew members aboard.

Miguel nodded. "They all know their job."

"As long as we can get everybody off before sundown." Port Authority only worked in daylight for this kind of situation. The chances for mistakes increased in the evening, and nobody wanted that.

"We will." Miguel paused. "I'll go oversee the crew. You find Miss Clark."

Matias ran a hand over the back of his neck. "Do you know where she is?"

Miguel tipped his chin toward the other staircase. "In the restaurant." He took the lists from Matias. "Good luck."

"Funny guy," Matias said as Miguel climbed the stairs. He blew out a breath. How was he going to say goodbye to Vanessa?

After the activity of the past few hours, the calm and solitude in the restaurant was a welcome change. The last few rays of sun filtered in through the curtains on the windows and the whole room glowed with an eerie solitude.

An empty ship always caught him by surprise, as if the passengers and crew were only momentarily gone. Rooms usually emptied on the last day, but this trip had already broken all the rules. One more exception didn't make much difference.

Vanessa sat at the farthest table to the port side,

under a single spotlight. When she met his eyes, her lips widened into a smile. His heart tripped.

He'd missed her. He'd missed her voice and her smile and the way her hand fit in his. How many times had they held hands? He couldn't remember, but there hadn't been many. Only enough to know he missed it already.

Her braided hair had loosened as the day wore on, and wisps brushed the side of her face and neck. Her smile was genuine, but fatigue lined her expression. He'd heard from Afonso and Miss Rialto that Vanessa had helped all afternoon, and he wanted to take her in his arms and thank her in kisses.

Instead, Matias took his time walking over—time to watch her, time to think about what he wanted to say. They were due a conversation, and he had no idea how it would turn out. What if it didn't go well? He didn't even have her phone number. He wiped his palms along the sides of his pants.

He pulled out a chair and turned it around. "Thank you for everything you did today. Are you ready? We don't have much time left."

She shrugged. "Maybe."

That was not the answer he'd been waiting for. Matias rose an eyebrow. "Maybe what?"

She turned her phone screen down on the white tablecloth. "I called Grandfather."

Her eyes shone with some kind of excitement. He'd expected her to be more regretful to see the cruise end in this manner.

"Of course he already knew about everything going on here, as I knew he would. But I have to say he was very surprised at the reason for my call. He recovered quickly and approved my idea."

"You have an idea that your grandfather likes? I thought—" He clamped his mouth. Vanessa's relationship with her grandfather was none of his business.

She leaned over in his direction and Matias straightened. It was a new experience for him, having someone he was so attracted to so near and knowing he should keep his distance instead.

Her voice lowered. "You thought I don't get along with Grandfather." She hunched a shoulder. "Well, things change, and people do too."

Matias struggled with a reply. People did change even when the change was not an expected one.

"Do you know what happened to the ship?"

Her change of topic confused him for a moment, but he recovered quickly. "We lost the rudder. Without the ability to turn, the ship drifted into a sandbank." It had been a stroke of luck to hit the soft sand instead of a jagged rock. The result would have been much different.

"Isn't the ship practically new? How do you lose a rudder?"

"There was a part that sustained some damage, and that affected the rudder. It's complicated."

She frowned. "If Grandfather had asked you the same question, would you have said that?"

"Well, no. He knows the ship and the parts that it comprises." Senhor Valadares worked closely with the designers and was always involved in the construction process. Matias had seen him before on the construction dock.

"Then explain it to me the same way."

Matias crossed his forearms over the back of the chair. "Vanessa, I need to get you off the ship. All the other passengers have been evacuated already."

After a pause, she met his eyes. "I'm not like the other passengers."

She was right, of course. But he still had to follow the protocol, whether she liked it or not. Matias stood. "Please, Vanessa. You need to go. They're transferring the crew right now, and they won't wait for you after that."

"It's all right, Matias. I'm not transferring to the other ship."

"Say that again?"

Vanessa reached out and touched his forearm. "Matias, hear me out. I want to stay aboard and follow the ship back to port."

"There are rules and procedures for this kind of thing, and I'm the captain. I can't go around making exceptions."

"You can if the company's president approves."

Matias didn't even try to hide his surprise. "He approves? Your grandfather approves of you staying aboard instead of transferring to the *Alma Vida*?"

Vanessa folded her arms. "I thought you'd be happier about having me aboard for a little longer."

"And I thought you didn't want anything to do with this ship." Even as he said that to her, the idea of having her around turned in his mind. He shook his head. "Everyone's leaving except me, the engineer, and the mechanic. I don't know when the tow boat will be here or how long it'll take to tow us to port. Why do you want to stay aboard?"

"What if I say I want to spend more time with you?" She reached for her phone. "Here, I'll have you talk to Grandfather."

She wanted to stay for him? By the time he recovered enough to reply, she was already making her call.

"Yes, he's right here." She held out her phone in Matias's direction.

Matias took it. "This is Captain Romano."

Vanessa feigned an interest in her nails.

"Captain, you and your crew did an amazing job evacuating the passengers," Senhor Valadares said. "I know this is never the kind of situation we want, but congratulations on a job well done."

"Thank you, sir." He cleared his throat. "Sir, your granddaughter wants to stay aboard until the *Princess Catarina* gets to port."

"Captain, a word of advice. When a woman changes her mind in your favor, you don't ask why; you say thank you."

Matias didn't know what to reply to that. He rubbed his temple with his free hand. "Yes, sir. As long as you're okay with this arrangement."

"I am. I'm also sending two of my men to be on hand, just in case. I'll see you at port, Captain."

Matias returned the phone to Vanessa. The hope and assurance in her eyes were hard to resist. They still hadn't talked about the kiss—the one he hadn't been able to keep at the back of his mind like he should. Just the memory of her caramel-flavored lips was enough to flush his neck. He'd never think of the flan pudding dessert in the same way again.

Matias let out a long breath. "Since you're staying, let's go over some rules. Rule number one: you do what the captain says."

Her face split into a smile. "Yes, captain." She straightened in her chair and mock saluted him, then quickly sobered up. "So tell me how the accident happened. I thought the ship had ways to prevent accidents."

He looked straight at her. "It wasn't an accident."

Vanessa turned at the sound of the sliding door as Matias stepped onto the balcony off the lounge. The water lapped gently against the hull and the moonlight glinted in the long waves of the river.

He switched off the overhead light and the low-lights came on along the edge of the floor. With a waxing moon climbing steadily in the dark sky, the ambient light was enough in the small space. The air was balmy and the night calm, its soundtrack the nocturnal noises of insects on the banks and the occasional chatter from the small crew of the Port Authority boat.

With the tow ship scheduled to arrive in the early morning, Vanessa had the whole night ahead to keep Matias company. She'd be content to just sit next to him and not worry with anything else, but when would she have another chance like this to talk to him?

She looked up at him. "Is everything okay?"

He'd gone to the lower deck to check on the mechanic and the engineer.

Matias sat on the double chair next to her. "Yes, everything's fine. They already had dinner too."

With a kitchen full of dishes for a dinner that never got served, Matias and Vanessa had taken some food to the Port Authority crew members and then had a laid-back dinner in the restaurant.

An unnatural quiet had settled over the ship. Vanessa had grown used to the sounds of conversation and music from the previous nights on the trip. Tonight, the silence echoed in each room and she struggled to reconcile the new reality.

"It's hard to believe the cruise ended this way." She sat back and watched Matias's profile.

Matias stretched his arms and folded his hands behind his neck. "It is."

He didn't add more to his reply, and there was a faraway look in his eyes. The wariness in his voice belied the tension he was trying hard to hide from her.

Vanessa turned in her seat to face him. "Why did you say earlier that the damage wasn't an accident?"

"Because what we saw downstairs points at deliberate sabotage."

"And you know this for sure?"

"I'd be very surprised if the investigators came to a different conclusion." He sat up and positioned his hands to indicate a small object. "It's like this. The ship's rudder facilitates the steering. This rudder is controlled by hydraulics which are in turn controlled by a compressor, and the compressor has an electric regulator."

"All the parts are connected," she said. Even if she didn't know the specifics, it was simple enough to understand so far.

Matias nodded. "Yes, it all works together. That's how a ship works. Unfortunately, it also makes it easier to inflict damage. We found evidence that someone planted a timed device that fried the regulator. Without the regulator, the hydraulics were compromised, and the rudder became useless."

She frowned. "Then someone aboard did it." Either a passenger or a crew member had purposefully sabotaged the ship. "But why? And who?"

"I don't know." He passed a hand through his hair. "That will be a job for the investigators. My job now is to make sure the evidence is not destroyed."

"Is that why the mechanic and the engineer are in lower deck?" It all made sense.

"We took pictures and secured the room, but yes, they're keeping an eye on it until the ship arrives at port and the investigators take over."

For a man who knew someone aboard his ship had betrayed him, Matias looked calm and in control. How much of it was a façade and how much his personality?

"You don't seem very worried," she said.

"I've already done all I can for now. Worrying about something I can't control would only rob me of the ability to enjoy the present moment." The corner of his mouth rose into a small smile.

Vanessa's face flushed and she brushed at her cheek. Matias wasn't the only one enjoying the present moment. She'd never imagined she'd be sitting with the captain in a nearly empty ship.

Matias leaned back in his chair. "There's something I realized today. I've been doing this itinerary for some years and never have I had a trip with so many problems. It's been doomed from the beginning, even before we left port, each day adding something more to the list of malfunctions and accidents and overall difficulties to an unprecedented scale. And just when I thought it couldn't get any worse, we lose the rudder." He shook his head. "Ending the trip early is unheard of. I've never had to send the passengers ashore before the cruise was over."

His expression was heavy with disappointment.

"But this situation is out of your hands." Even if he felt responsible, he wasn't to blame for the sabotage.

"Of course I've also known from the beginning that you were the one who brought the bad luck aboard."

Vanessa's eyes went wide. What was he talking about? She had no words; nothing came to mind to defend herself from his insensitive remarks. How had she brought any bad luck to the ship?

He turned his palm up, as if reading from a list. "I looked at that passenger manifest on the first day, saw the uneven number of passengers, and knew that someone traveling alone was not a good portent on a cruise for couples."

Vanessa rose and walked to the railing, turning away from Matias. Her eyes stung, and she blinked in a futile attempt to hold back the tears. Her heart sank. Why was he blaming her for something that was out of her control? As if she had anything to do with any of the problems that had besieged the ship. How had he gone from talking about the ship's rudder to accusing her of bringing bad luck?

She had to leave. Right now.

"I don't have to stay here and listen to this." She walked away from him as fast as she could, but he caught her arm.

"Vanessa, wait. Please. I'm an idiot." His hand slid down her wrist until his fingers touched hers. "Here I am trying to tell you how I don't care for the silly old superstitions anymore and I manage to insult you instead."

She didn't turn, continuing to face away from him, but she was caught in place by the gentle pressure of his hand in hers. When he stepped forward, the warmth of his body hovered at her back. Now she was torn between the urge to flee and the need to stay close to him. She leaned back ever so lightly, and his hand came to rest at her waist, then his chin rested on her shoulder.

Vanessa closed her eyes and took a deep breath.

"I'm sorry," he repeated. "What I'm trying to say is, I'm so lucky to know you and so glad your grandfather sent you on this cruise. I'm especially glad you came unattached and are not part of a couple." His hand tightened around her waist. "So lucky," he said in a soft voice.

His breath fanned her neck and her skin turned into gooseflesh.

This is what she'd been wishing to hear from him.

Slowly, she turned in his arms until she faced him. Matias brought her closer and touched the side of her face with a feathery kiss. Her chest felt like it would burst into flames, and her knees struggled to support her shaking frame.

"Matias." Her voice trembled, thick with emotion, and she paused to inhale. All the questions tumbling in her mind—she didn't want to think of them right now. Not when time was so short.

"Forgive me for those stupid words, please?" He touched her lips again. "You're the best thing that's happened to me in a long, long time. I don't care about even numbers on the passenger list."

Vanessa tightened her arms around his waist and rested her head against his shoulder. She closed her eyes. What could she say to Matias when she didn't know what to think? Was it even possible to become so close to another person in such a short period of time? She was caught between the voice of reason in her mind and the yearnings of the feelings in her heart.

Knowing which one to listen to wasn't as easy as she would like.

CHAPTER SEVENTEEN

*V*anessa woke with a deep exhale. A sense of contentment filled her chest, something new and unexpected. When was the last time she'd woken to such a feeling?

Outside, a trace of night still clung to the sky, stubbornly pushing away the early morning light. Morning could wait. Let the rest of darkness linger on and take its time to fade.

A warm breath fanned her cheek. She lay in the cocoon of Matias's arms, the weight of one across her waist and the other around her shoulders. How they had managed to get any sleep while in each other's embrace baffled her. Maybe the trust and caring between them was deeper than what they consciously knew.

After their time on the balcony, they'd come inside and ended up on the widest sofa in the lounge, large

195

enough for the both of them. They'd talked of little things, not really minding where the words took them as long as they stayed next to each other. In the end, the tiredness of the day exacted its toll, and here she was now, awake, as Matias slept, the little wrinkle between his brows finally gone.

Vanessa covered his hand with hers and closed her eyes for a moment. The little question that had niggled her the day before crept in once again. Was this the kind of happiness to last a lifetime and beyond? How could she know what was true and enduring in such a short period of time? And how could she make a choice?

If she stayed in Portugal, Grandfather would be pleased and so would Matias, but she'd be leaving Dad and the only life she'd ever known. And by returning to Kansas, she'd be closing the door on her Portuguese family and rejecting the possibility of a relationship with Matias, breaking her own heart in the process.

As the minutes wore on, Vanessa wavered on the edge of indecision, going back and forth between her choices, the impossibility of each growing larger and heavier. The comfort she took from being close to Matias would only bring heartache and, in the end, whichever path she chose would end in sorrow.

On the floor somewhere, her phone beeped. Slowly, she removed Matias's arm and stood from the sofa as stealthily as she could. Let him sleep. He needed the rest.

Vanessa exited the lounge and swiped at the phone screen. Dad's number flashed back at her. She quickly calculated the time in Kansas. Why was he calling her so late?

"Dad, is something wrong?"

"Hi, Vanessa." His voice sounded tired. "Nothing wrong. Just wanted to let you know I just landed at the Porto airport."

Her stomach dropped. "You're in Porto? What are you doing in Porto?" Had he mentioned anything about coming and she'd missed it?

"I didn't like the way we ended our last phone call, so I wanted to surprise you. Are you still on the ship?"

"I am." This was not the time to explain what was going on with the ship. "Where are you staying?"

"Some hotel in the city, I don't remember the name. How soon can you get here? I'd like to see you."

Typical Dad, expecting her to drop everything to accommodate his plans. A feeling of resentment flared for a moment. Vanessa breathed in and pushed it away. Maybe this was the chance she needed to confront Dad about the truth about her past and about Mom. "I'll see what I can do. I'll text you when I know for sure."

His voice brightened. "That's my girl. I'll send you the name of the place where I'm staying. See you soon."

Vanessa hung up and sat on the carpeted hallway floor. In the course of five minutes, everything had changed. Only a few moments before, she'd been considering turning away from him, the parent who'd raised her and who'd been the only family she'd had growing up.

Now Dad was in Porto and he wanted to see her. Maybe this was her answer.

She rose from the floor and walked back to where Matias still lay sleeping on the sofa. His breathing was deep and his expression relaxed, almost smiling.

It was all wishful thinking, this alternate reality with Matias. Thinking she could have a happily-ever-after with him was only a fairy tale—nothing more than a beautiful dream.

Quickly, Vanessa walked back to her cabin to call Grandfather.

Then it was time to wake Matias.

"Matias."

Someone called his name. Matias smiled. The soft voice in his dream sounded like Vanessa. Even the sweet accent was the same. And the way she said the S at the end—he loved that.

"Matias."

This time he opened his eyes. It wasn't a dream.

When he took a look around, Matias found himself on a sofa instead of the bed in his cabin. He sat up and leaned back against the seat. After their talk out on the balcony, he and Vanessa had gone inside and sat on a sofa in the lounge. Had he slept there all night? And where had Vanessa slept? A hazy image of holding her in his arms flashed through his mind. Was it a memory or had he imagined it?

Vanessa sat across from him on an upholstered chair. A small smile tugged at the corner of her lips, but her shoulders hunched over, her arms crossed over her middle. Her expression was heavy with worry and frustration, and even a little sadness.

He scrubbed a hand across his face, then straightened. "What's wrong?" Outside, morning hadn't come yet; a few stubborn stars still clung to a dusky sky.

She followed his gaze past the windows. "I'm sorry I woke you up so early."

An undertone of regret tinged her voice. Something inside him twisted with a sense of premonition. "Vanessa, what's going on?" What was she keeping from him? She barely maintained eye contact, and she had ignored his question as well.

She inhaled deeply and closed her eyes for a moment, as if to breathe in the courage she lacked. When she opened them again, the resolve was there. "I'm leaving. I know I said I was staying until the *Princess Catarina* was towed to port, but I have to go."

For the length of a heartbeat, Matias stared at her. He scrambled for a reply, but the words failed him. Why had she changed her mind?

Vanessa stood. "I'm going to find my suitcase and then go. My dad is waiting for me at a hotel in Porto."

"You dad?" His forehead wrinkled into a frown. "Your dad's here in Portugal?" Matias rose from the sofa.

Her head cocked to the side, and she hunched a shoulder. "It's a long story."

The realization sneaked in and grew until it was impossible to ignore. Vanessa was running away. She was ready to leave the ship and she wouldn't even say why.

A horn sounded from outside, loud and insistent.

"That's for me." She glanced at him for a moment. "I'm sorry to leave you, but the Port Authority captain said the tow ship will be here in less than an hour."

That was the only good news he'd heard so far. He was anxious to turn his ship over to the company's investigators.

They stood in front of each other for a long minute until Vanessa broke eye contact. "Thank you, Matias." Her gaze flicked back. "I know that's hardly enough..." Her words trailed off.

Every thought he had rushed around in his mind, but none of them connected in any rational way. The situation happening in front of him didn't make any sense, but he didn't know what he could say to make it different.

When the horn sounded again, Vanessa squared her shoulders. "Goodbye, Matias."

By the time he recovered, she was already climbing the stairs to the upper deck. Matias followed as she handed her suitcase to a guy he'd never seen before.

He walked over and stopped by the railing. "That's it? Goodbye?" There was so much more he wanted to ask.

Vanessa looked over her shoulder. "I think we both know it wouldn't have worked."

No, they didn't know that. And now they never would.

Vanessa wiped at the corner of her eye once more. It was more of a persistent leak than crying. A very annoying leak that wouldn't stop. After a night spent in Matias's arms and then waking up early and weighing her options, she'd made her decision. Then why was she crying?

Two of Grandfather's men had picked her up in a heavily tinted sedan, and she settled in for the trip back, grateful she didn't have to take a bus.

When she'd called Grandfather, the news of Dad's arrival in Porto had taken him by surprise, just as it had her. Dad hadn't even hinted that he was coming. As far as she knew, he hadn't been in Portugal since Mom's accident. And now he was waiting for her in Porto. She sighed heavily.

Fatigue overtook her on the hour-and-a-half drive back, and she dozed off. When they arrived at the hotel, Grandfather waited for her in the lobby.

He stood from the upholstered chair and rushed to her. "I'm sorry about this, Vanessa. I know you wanted to see the ship back to port."

"Where is he? Did you see him yet?" She walked over to the reception desk, but Grandfather stopped her.

"Are you sure you want to do this right now? I can take you back to the apartment, and he can wait until you're ready."

Grandfather had rented a small apartment with a fabulous view of the city for her. Had she even appreciated it? Other than hiding there, she hadn't done much.

She shook her head. "No, I'd rather see him first."

He hesitated for a moment, as if weighing her answer, then gestured to the elevators. "Come on."

Vanessa managed a small smile. "Thanks, Grandfather." Her resentment toward him had faded after reading the letter he'd given her two days ago. So many things had happened on the cruise. She wasn't the same person she'd been before boarding the ship.

When she knocked on the door, Dad swung it open. "Vanessa. Finally." He pulled her into the room and dropped an arm around her shoulders.

Vanessa returned the hug. "Hi, Dad. This is quite the surprise."

He and Grandfather nodded curtly at each other with an undercurrent of tension that was hard to ignore.

"Why didn't you tell me you were coming, Dad?" Vanessa walked over to the sofa and sat down.

Dad sat across from her. "Just wanted to see how you were doing."

"We talked on the phone and texted almost every day." He'd done it so often, she'd been forced to leave her phone behind in her cabin at times. "I'm twenty-three. Don't you think I can take care of myself by now?"

Dad crossed his arms. "Of course I know you can take care of yourself. Just because you're twenty-three doesn't mean I'll stop worrying about you."

"You knew where I was, Dad." The weariness she felt tinged her voice. "I was perfectly well the whole time."

Grandfather turned from his spot at the window but didn't say anything.

"I wouldn't call it perfectly well. Didn't the boat get stuck in the middle of the river?"

"Ship, not boat," she and Grandfather spoke at the same time.

Dad stood up from his chair and gestured between her and Grandfather. "See, this is the kind of thing I tried to prevent. You spend a few days on a ship, and already you're talking like him."

"And what's wrong about that? Maybe I want to learn from him about the ship." She stopped and tried to soften her tone. "I have a feeling it's what my mom would have wanted."

Dad stilled, his eyes wide. "Your mother? Now you're talking about your mother too?"

Vanessa leaned an elbow on the side of the chair. "At least somebody is." As tired as she was, some things needed to be said.

Dad frowned. "What's gotten into you? Why are you talking like that?"

"Well, Dad, maybe it's about time we talk like this." She uncrossed her legs and rose. "I didn't sleep well, I'm tired, I'm hungry, and I didn't plan for this conversation to take place right now, but frankly I don't care if you don't like it. I think it's high time we set everything straight."

Dad opened his mouth, but Vanessa cut him off. "And I'm making the rules as I go or as I see fit."

She'd never talked to Dad like this, and she hovered on the fine line between asserting herself and being rude. She was probably not making much sense, but she might as well keep going, now that she'd opened the door for this talk. "I'm sure you didn't come all this way to argue with me."

Dad waved a hand. "Since your trip didn't go as expected, I thought we could change your return ticket and you can leave a few days earlier with me. There's nothing else for you here."

Vanessa looked away and sighed. Did he even understand how wrong he was?

Grandfather looked over this shoulder at Vanessa. "It's up to you when you leave. You know you'll have a place to stay as long as you want."

Dad glanced at Grandfather, then back at her. "You don't have to listen to him, Vanessa."

"You're right. I don't have to listen to him, but I want to. He didn't lie to me like you did." Repeatedly. Dad had lied to her even when he didn't need to.

Dad crossed his arms. "If I lied, it was for your own good."

Her chest tightened. Years of frustration bubbled to the surface after holding in her questions for so long. "But why? You said she'd died in an accident but never gave me more details. You didn't even tell me her whole name." Vanessa paced away then turned back. "Something as simple as my mom's name, and you never told me."

Dad sat back down and pinched the bridge of his nose. "I wasn't myself after the boating accident. I lost your mom to the river, and I didn't want to lose you too." He looked back up at her. "Moving to Kansas City was a reaction, trying to get away from the ships and the river cruises and everything else that represented pain to me. I thought—" He paused, and his head went down. "I only did what I thought was best."

"You didn't even tell me I had family here." Vanessa gestured to Grandfather, who'd turned from the window and sat at the farthest chair. She'd been only three when Mom had died, and any memories she might have had were too fleeting to remember. "He had to wait until I was twenty-one to see me on an iPad, and Grandmother had to wait until I came here. How do you explain that, Dad?"

Vanessa walked to the window and squeezed her eyes shut for a moment. Even if he'd had the best intentions, the result of Dad's very one-sided decision had affected more than himself and his child. Over twenty years later, the repercussions had a heavier impact in their lives than he could have predicted. What could she do to move forward from this situation? She was a grown woman now, one who could make new decisions and try to repair some of the damage done.

She unclenched her hands and took a deep breath, then another. When she turned around from the window, both men looked at her. One whom she knew and had grown up with; the other, someone whom she longed to know better, someone who could tell her more about the mother she didn't remember. So much of her past and her present intertwined.

And what of her future? For the first time in a long while, she didn't have anything planned—not for the week or even the rest of the month.

She was open and free to all the possibilities.

Her expression softened. "Dad, I think it's time you let me decide what I want to do."

Dad looked at her and, after a moment, nodded at last. "What are you going to do then?"

Vanessa offered him a small smile. "Would you like me to show you around Porto before you leave?

CHAPTER EIGHTEEN

$\mathcal{M}$atias approached the reception desk. "Captain Romano to see Senhor Valadares."

The secretary nodded at him and lifted her phone. "Captain Romano's here, sir." She put the phone down. "He's ready for you, Captain."

Matias thanked her and walked down the hallway flanked with floor to ceiling windows. The view from the twentieth floor on a hill opened to the city before him and reminded him of the reasons he loved Porto so much. Below, down the river, three of the company's ships lined in a single file, the *Princess Catarina* at the rear, floating unperturbed on an early autumn day. How were the repairs coming along?

The folder weighed in his hand, a reminder of his failure in his position over the *Princess Catarina* during the most recent trip. He still didn't have all the facts about what had happened, but hopefully he'd get some answers of his own today.

It had been a while since his last visit to the Gold River company's main office. And this would be the last.

He'd tried to come the day after arriving at port with the towed ship, but after a brief interview with the investigators, he'd received a message rescheduling his meeting with Senhor Valadares. It had given him the time to write a detailed report of the trip. His version, anyways. Maybe not 100 percent accurate, but to the best of his knowledge. After reading his own words, he'd also included a resignation letter. As hard as it had been to write it, it was the right thing to do. It was time to move on.

Vanessa had come and gone from his life in the same manner, one day there and one day gone. They'd never gotten around to exchanging contact information; he'd been too busy with the accidents aboard, and he didn't think to ask until after she was gone. Was she still in the country, or had she returned home with her father? As much as he tried, he couldn't stop thinking about her.

When he knocked on the door, Senhor Valadares opened it himself. "Captain Romano. Thanks for coming to see me." He shook Matias's hand.

Matias quickly assessed Senhor Valadares— the wide smile, the friendly voice and bright eyes. Not what Matias had expected after the events of the last trip. For sure, Senhor Valadares would change his demeanor after reading Matias' report.

"How are you, sir?" He walked over to the desk and placed the folder on the surface.

Senhor Valadares sat down and indicated the chair across from the desk. "I'm doing well. What's this?" He reached for the folder.

"My report of last week's trip. And my letter of resignation."

Senhor Valadares frowned as he opened the folder and scanned the papers. "Letter of resignation? You got a better offer? From whom?"

Matias stared at Senhor Valadares. "A better offer? No, nobody has offered me a job." And nobody would after word got out.

"Then why are you resigning?"

"It's all in the report, sir." Matias gestured at the stack of papers in the folder. "I'm taking full responsibility for what happened."

Senhor Valadares arched an eyebrow. "Are you saying you're responsible for the sabotage?"

"No, sir, but as the captain it's my duty to be aware of what goes on aboard my ship, and I failed."

Senhor Valadares watched him for a moment. "I can see why you'd feel that way, but you're not responsible for the damage to the hydraulics." He reached in a drawer and handed Matias a sheet of paper. "The preliminary report is in, Captain. As you suspected, the damage was purposeful sabotage."

Matias scanned the report. It lacked the details that would come in the comprehensive report, but the main causes were listed, just as he and the engineer had thought. "Are there any ideas as to the perpetrator?" He returned the report.

"Perpetrators. We don't have any concrete proof, but we suspect two crew members." He hesitated before going on. "What can you tell me about Anabela Rialto and Afonso Cortez?"

Matias's eyes widened. "They're suspects?" The surprise in his voice was hard to hold back. "I can tell you only good things about either one. Anabela is one of the best cruise directors I've worked with and Afonso always behaved professionally as a pianist and emergency response specialist." Matias paused, thinking of all he knew of his former crew members. "Why would they do this? It doesn't make any sense."

"We don't know all the reasons yet. The investigation is ongoing and it will take some time to unravel everything. As part of the initial inquiry, we requested interviews with each member of the crew. These two disappeared and we couldn't locate them. Then two days ago Afonso Cortez came forward with very specific information about the sabotage and his and Anabela Rialto's involvement."

"What kind of involvement, if I may ask?"

"She's mainly responsible for several accidents aboard plus the sabotage to the hydraulics. Afonso Cortez knew of her plans and didn't tell anyone or try to stop her. He'll be prosecuted accordingly, but so far his story corroborates, and there's enough evidence to support he's telling the truth. Just wish he'd done it sooner."

Matias did too. He was glad to know there was an explanation for the accidents that happened aboard, but he still had so many questions. "Do you know where Miss Rialto is?"

"Not yet, but I have a private investigator tracking her down."

More than seeing justice served, closure to the case was important as well.

Senhor Valadares picked up the resignation letter. "Captain, let's talk about this letter."

"Yes, sir." Matias straightened in his chair.

"What do you say we forget you brought it in?" Senhor Valadares pushed the paper across the desk to Matias.

Matias looked at the paper but didn't move to pick it up. He hesitated for only a second before going on. "Sir, even though I wasn't directly involved with any of the accidents or sabotage, I still feel it was my responsibility to have been more aware. The truth is, I let myself be distracted with my growing feelings for your granddaughter."

Senhor Valadares raised an eyebrow. "I was the one who asked you to watch Vanessa. Did you neglect any of your duties as a captain?"

"No, sir. I delegated to other crew members who effectively carried out my orders whenever I couldn't be present."

"Did you personally see to Vanessa's safety?"

"I did, but I'm afraid I may have enjoyed my time with her on a more personal level than what you had in mind."

Senhor Valadares's mouth rose in a small smile. "Don't apologize, Captain Romano. From where I stand, falling for Vanessa was inevitable, even if I am a little biased."

Matias frowned. "Are you saying you're okay with it?"

"You're both adults and unattached, aren't you?" He picked up the letter of resignation and handed it to Matias.

Matias held it for a moment before folding it and slipping it in this pocket. He wasn't about to argue again.

Senhor Valadares stood and came around his desk. "Why don't you go home and enjoy the rest of your leave? We'll have plenty of time to discuss the rest when you return."

"I'll do that, sir," Matias said and shook Senhor Valadares's hand. "Sir, if I may ask after your granddaughter?"

Senhor Valadares rubbed his chin. "My granddaughter." He settled a hand on Matias's shoulder. "You haven't heard from her?"

"No, sir. I don't have her phone number and she doesn't have mine."

"I'll pass yours along then. I'm sure you understand that's all I can do. The rest is up to her."

Matias would have preferred to have Vanessa's number. What if she didn't call? Would he wait a week, a month before tracking down her number and calling her himself? He would have to do something about it if it came to that.

"One more thing, Captain." Senhor Valadares stopped at the door. "I know you're on leave, but we're hiring for a new cruise director and the hiring manager is conducting interviews on the *Princess Catarina*. I'd love to have your impressions on the candidate."

Was that how they hired cruise directors? Matias hadn't been part of the process last time. "Of course, sir. That won't be a problem. I'll send you an email later today."

Senhor Valadares smiled. "Perfect."

Matias walked down to the dock instead of driving there. Parking was always at a premium by the river front, and despite the cooler temperatures and partially overcast sky, he craved the exercise to help him sort through his thoughts. He still had a job, but he was no closer to knowing what had gone wrong with Vanessa, let alone sorting his feelings for her. For a man used to taking the reins and not waiting for anyone else, patience took time to learn.

When Matias arrived, the repair crew had a truck parked in front of the gangway, but he didn't find any other cars in the vicinity. He climbed aboard on the sun deck and then descended to the upper deck. The reception desk was unmanned, and in the lounge all the furniture had been pushed to the side. Clear vinyl runners covered the carpet in the main areas, and cleaning workers darted in and out of cabins in the hallways. He greeted them, but after a few minutes of walking around, he still didn't come across anyone conducting interviews for the position of cruise director.

His phone rang. An unknown local number flashed on his screen. He didn't recognize it, but it could be one of his cousins who'd heard Matias was back in town. He still hadn't checked in with Jacinta. After a moment of hesitation, Matias answered the call.

"Hello?"

A familiar soft voice with an American accent came on. "Matias, it's me."

Matias gripped his phone tighter and held a breath. "Vanessa."

"Grandfather gave me your phone number."

"He did? I mean, I can see he did." What an idiotic answer. Of course her grandfather had given her his number. He was on the phone with her right now. His mouth split into a grin even as his heart somersaulted inside his chest—she hadn't waited to call him.

"I was wondering if we could meet."

His reply was immediate. "Yes. Tell me where." If she was back in Kansas, he'd go there. He'd go anywhere.

"Will you meet me at the bridge of the *Princess Catarina*?"

214

At the sound of galloping steps up the ladder, Vanessa turned around. Grandfather had given her Matias's phone number and waiting was not even an option; she'd called Matias right away. And here he was, practically running toward her with the widest smile on his face.

He wore dark jeans and a V-neck sweater over a buttondown shirt, with trimmed, stylish stubble on his face and his hair rumpled from the morning breeze. He looked so different from the smooth-faced, uniformed captain she'd grown to know, and yet his warm expression was familiar and dear to her.

Matias approached her and grinned. "Vanessa. Hi."

She smiled back, not knowing how to greet him. A handshake? A kiss on the cheek like they did here in Portugal? She definitely wanted more than that. They both held back from a gesture and smiled at each other instead.

They walked around the bridge and stopped at the railing over the prow. The memories rushed back of all the moments they'd spent there.

For a moment, Matias slipped his hands in his pockets but then shook his head and reached for one of her hands.

Vanessa stepped closer and grabbed on to his fingers. "I'm going to miss seeing you in uniform."

He chuckled. "There goes my charisma."

"As if you have anything to worry about."

He kept his eyes on her, a lopsided smile on his lips. "I thought you went back to Kansas with your father."

Vanessa released a deep breath. "No. I showed him around Porto, and he finally told me about my mother." She'd learned about the accident that had taken not only Mom's life, but also other crew members of a day-trip boat, a short voyage that had turned deadly due to human error.

"I took him to the airport last night." She swallowed past the nervous lump in her throat, her heart thumping faster when Matias squeezed her fingers. "I needed time to think."

He nodded. "I did too. But I missed you nonetheless."

She'd missed him as well. The past few days away from him had given her the clarity to understand what she wanted. "When is your next trip?"

Matias smiled. "Not for a while. I'm on leave." He gestured at the ship around them. "They need to finish some repairs anyways."

She raised an eyebrow and smiled. "So what are you doing here? Do you like to spend your time off aboard the ship as well?"

"Your grandfather asked me to sit in on the interview for a new cruise director but I haven't seen anyone around yet."

It was Vanessa's turn to chuckle. "Grandfather." She playfully rolled her eyes. "I don't know if I should get mad at him for interfering or thank him instead."

Matias frowned. "What did he interfere with?"

"My new job. Well, potential job." At Matias's continued confusion, she offered him a little clue.

"I heard you'll be needing a new cruise director."

His eyes widened. "You're the new cruise director?"

She hurried on to explain. "Not yet. I'll be training through the winter. I have so much to learn. Not only about the job but the language and everything else." So many new responsibilities. She also wanted to learn more about Mom, her grandparents, and the rest of her extended family. Even herself. "And I need to check with the captain to see if he approves."

Matias replied without hesitation. "The captain approves. Wholeheartedly." He hugged her tightly.

When Vanessa tilted up for a kiss, Matias took her face in his hands and kissed her without holding back. Her heart flipped as all the emotions rushed through her.

No more hesitations. No more questions. Only the sweetest feeling of rightness.

He slipped his arms around her waist and Vanessa leaned back to look at him. "We never did meet for the sunrise on the last day of the trip."

Matias met her gaze. "I have a feeling we'll have a thousand sunrises together."

ACKNOWLEDGMENTS

*E*very time I think I know what I'm doing, I get a project that challenges me.

Such was the case with this story. Matias and Vanessa came to me, hesitant at first, and I struggled a lot in the beginning. It didn't help that I was ill when I started writing, but I had enough faith to keep going, and I'm glad I did. I love how their story turned out!

Along the way, several people helped me get there and I want to thank them here: Amber and Jolene for the brainstorming help; Lindzee, for running with the series idea; my editors, Michele Holmes and Haley Swan; Michael for the ship damage scenario; and my great critique partners, Laura, Sally, and Lori, who hung in there with me almost pretty much everyday.

Last, but not least, thanks to my Mom for giving me the idea of a river cruise and then sponsoring a real one when I went to visit her (it was a one-day

cruise instead of the eight days, but still very lovely).
Obrigada!

Thank you for helping me share Matias and Vanessa's story with the world.

DEAR READER,

Thank you so much for reading Matias and Vanessa's story, *Meet Me at Sunrise*. I hope you've enjoyed reading it as much as I enjoyed writing it. You may learn more about them and their story on Pinterest.

Please consider leaving a review on Amazon and Goodreads. This is the best way to support me as an author.

For news of upcoming books and promotions, join my readers club.

I love to hear from readers! You can email me at lucinda@lucindawhitney.com.

Thank you!

Want to find out how Knox and Jacinta met?

Turn the page to read *Hold Me at Twilight*.

Read Knox and Jacinta's story
in *Hold Me at Twilight*.

CHAPTER ONE

$\mathcal{K}$nox shifted his backpack and straightened. This had to be the place. Only one person occupied the store front across the street, a young woman with brown hair. He checked his information, confirming the address and the name of the business. Even if the regular agent wasn't in today, he still had to take care of the issue. After the day he'd had, he was ready for a good meal and a long night's rest. But even that was out of his reach until he filed a police report.

The travel agency nestled in a small space decorated with brightly colored posters of local popular attractions, and the window was dressed with gold letters and a garland of clear mini lights along the casing. His one-week business trip to Porto, Portugal, had kept him busy during the first few days, leaving no time for sightseeing. But the training had gone well, and he'd found himself with free afternoons and evenings on the last three days, and out of ideas of what to do and how to use his time wisely.

After asking around, one of the Portuguese guys he'd worked with had recommended a local travel agency. Knox sent an email requesting ideas and the helpful agent had given him suggestions for events, trips, and points of interest. She'd also helped him figure out the train and bus schedules inside the city.

On impulse, at the end of the first sight-seeing day, he'd emailed her back to thank her, remarking on what he'd done that day. She'd replied the next morning with tips and more places to visit. They repeated the exchange for the next few days and he'd thanked her for making his time more enjoyable during his stay in Porto.

Several times she'd offered to help with anything else he might need, and he was just about to put that offer to the test.

When the light turned green, he joined the other pedestrians and crossed the street. Two older women chatted in front of the store window and when he paused by the door, they stopped and eyed him for a moment. Knox went in.

The young woman stood from her desk and said something in Portuguese.

Not again. Knox raised his shoulders. "I'm sorry, but I only speak English."

"That won't be a problem. What can I help you with?"

A temporary rush of relief came over him. Her friendly voice and ability to communicate filled him with gratitude. He felt the absurd desire to hug her but wisely resisted.

She glanced at the wall behind him.

Knox turned to find an ornamental clock with folk paintings of Portuguese icons. "You probably have an appointment and here I am barging in. I'll try to be brief."

She came around the desk. "No, I don't have any more appointments today, but we'll be closing soon."

The two older women who'd been on the sidewalk entered the agency and the woman's smile faltered. She said something to them in a very fast cadence, and they waved her off and sat on the two chairs along the wall. What was that about? Did she know them?

Knox turned back to the agent. "I had a J. Romano help me earlier in the week." He paused. This was turning more awkward than he'd anticipated. "Something came up and I could use some help today."

"I'm J. Romano. Are you a client of ours?"

It was her then. The woman before him with striking brown eyes and gorgeous dark hair also went out of her way to help others. His heart felt lighter. She'd made his trip so much more enjoyable. Well, up until last night, but that was completely unrelated.

He stepped forward. "Yes, I'm Knox Campbell. We exchanged emails this week."

Her eyes widened. "You're Mr. Campbell?"

"In the flesh." He grinned at her.

"I wasn't expecting someone so—" She studied him briefly, but recovered quickly. "I'm sorry. I'm being extremely rude. What can I do for you, Mr. Campbell?" Her expression softened in a gentle smile.

Knox hesitated. Someone so what? What had she been about to say?

"Did you extend your trip?" She asked, before he got a chance to reply. "I seem to remember that you were leaving today."

He'd be home by now if he'd left as planned. Maybe not that far, but at least closer to landing in New Jersey. "Well, about that." He blew out a breath. "Someone stole my wallet last night."

She gasped. The women on the chairs asked her something and she replied to them quickly. When they started talking in excited tones, she shushed them.

She turned back to him. "I'm sorry. You were saying your wallet got stolen? How awful." Her face was very expressive, her eyes full of sympathy for his situation.

Knox's ears heated. If it had been only his wallet. "My wallet with all my credit cards, my ID, and my passport." He confessed.

"Oh, no." Her eyes widened. "That must be so inconvenient for you."

Inconvenient was not a strong enough word to describe it.

One of the women stood and Miss Romano stopped her with a raised hand. The woman sat back down.

"Are these clients waiting to talk to you?" Knox looked at the women and they smiled at him.

"They're not clients." She glanced at them sternly and the women quieted down. "Have you been to the police yet? What did they say?"

Knox dragged his attention back from the exchange between the travel agent and the women. "Yes and no." He rubbed the side of his neck. "I went to the police station, but that didn't work out too well. I was hoping you could come with me and help me file the report with the officer on duty."

She stared at him.

"Just to facilitate the translation."

"Oh, yes. They don't always have someone there who can speak English."

He'd found that out the hard way. It seemed that every other Portuguese spoke English until he'd needed one. Then, of course, he couldn't find anyone who knew enough of the language to help translate his report.

The older women rose from their seats and approached Knox and Miss Romano. Knox stepped back.

Miss Romano sighed. "Excuse me, please."

In hushed tones, she conversed with the women who gestured in his direction several times. Miss Romano shook her head more than once, but in the end she relented to whatever they'd asked and spoke to them for a few moments longer. Whoever they were, they acted like they knew the travel agent personally and not just through business.

Were they trying to talk her out of helping him? What was he going to do if she changed her mind about coming with him to the police?

Of all the days to have Mãe and Tia Mariana show up to go home with her, this was not a good one. They came by a few times a week so they could walk home together with Jacinta. Depending on the day, she either appreciated it or wished they'd give her some room. Today would have been better if they'd skipped the visit.

"He's such a nice looking young man, Jacinta," Mom said again.

"And his eyes are so beautiful." Tia Mariana was partial to blue-eyed young men.

"He's a client and you two have to be quiet, or I'll ask you to wait outside until I'm done helping him." Jacinta talked under breath while trying to keep her smile.

She sent them a look loaded with warning, hoping it would work for a few more minutes, then turned back to the client. Mr. Campbell was a surprise. She hadn't expected him to be this young. From his emails, she'd assumed he was an older man who'd need some guidance in a foreign city.

But he was young and good looking and had the bluest eyes she'd ever seen, and it was quite embarrassing that her mom and aunt wouldn't stop staring at him.

"So you just need me to come and interpret for you, Mr. Campbell?"

He shifted his attention from her mom and aunt who still stared at him very impolitely. "Please, call me Knox. And yes, that's all I need." Hesitation filled his eyes for a brief moment. "I realize this is out of the realm of your regular work as a travel agent, and I'll happily pay for your time. I'm hoping it won't take too long."

It most likely would take some time, considering the slow, laborious Portuguese bureaucracy. But she didn't want to dash his hopes and tell him otherwise unless she had to.

"I can certainly help you with that." As inconvenient as it would be to accompany him, she couldn't leave him to go to the police by himself when he'd come to ask her.

"Thank you so much," he said. When his expression bloomed in open relief, that was all the confirmation she needed to know she should help him.

She went around her desk. After saving several documents, she turned off the computer.

Mãe stood and approached her, with Tia Mariana on her heels. "What did you say that made him so happy?"

Jacinta flipped off the back lights. "He needs to file a police report and I'm going with him to help translate."

"Jacinta, that is so nice of you," Tia Mariana said with a huge smile in Mr. Campbell's direction.

Mãe nodded, her expression matching that of her sister-in-law.

Jacinta suppressed a sigh. These two were more than she could take at times. "Come on, I need to lock up," she said to them.

She addressed Mr. Campbell in English. "Mr. Campbell, let me introduce you to my mother, Celestina, and my aunt, Mariana. They're on their way home and just stopped by to say hello."

He shook their hands and smiled. "Olá."

Mãe and Tia Mariana started talking with him and he chuckled. "I'm afraid that's all I know."

Mr. Campbell excused himself, then stepped out and waited for her on the sidewalk.

"Are you going with him right now then?" Mãe asked her.

"Yes, I'm going now so he can get it done and move on. I'm sure he's anxious to get his wallet back, if at all possible."

Jacinta turned on the alarm and gently prodded her relatives out the door so she could lock up.

Tia Mariana stared at Mr. Campbell. "How soon will he go back to America?"

"I have no idea, Tia." Jacinta turned the key in the lock and slipped it into her purse. She pulled out her phone and googled the directions. "Mr. Campbell, the closest police station is about thirty minutes away on foot. Do you mind if we walk there?"

"I don't mind at all," he said lightly.

Tia Mariana turned to Mr. Campbell. "Why don't you come for dinner when you're done?" she said slowly and loudly.

His forehead wrinkled and he shrugged at Tia Mariana. "What did she say?"

"She invited you for dinner when you're done at the police station." Jacinta explained. She should have known Mãe and Tia Mariana wouldn't let Mr. Campbell leave without an invitation.

"What does the normal protocol say in a situation like this?" Mr. Campbell asked her.

"What protocol?"

"I read in a travel book about Portugal that it's impolite to turn down invitations. Is that true?"

Jacinta hid a chuckle behind her hand. "That's entirely up to you, Mr. Campbell. They'll survive if you turn them down."

He hesitated for a moment. "Would you tell her I'll have to wait and see how long it takes?"

Jacinta related back to Tia Mariana and Mãe, saying she'd keep them updated but making no promises. She couldn't gauge Mr. Campbell's reaction. Was he trying to politely get out of the invitation or did he want to go but was unsure of what Jacinta thought?

She said goodbye to her mom and aunt, then walked away in the opposite direction with Mr. Campbell beside her.

Did she want to bring him by for dinner? Tomorrow

was a holiday and a lot of the extended family would be at the house tonight.

How would he react to the crazy chaos of the Romano family?

Find *Hold Me at Twilight* on Amazon

THE AUTHOR

𝓛ucinda Whitney was born and raised in Portugal, where she received a Master's degree from the University of Minho in Braga, in Portuguese/English teaching.

She lives in northern Utah with her husband and four children. When she's not reading and writing, she can be found with a pair of knitting needles, or tending her herb garden.

She's the author of *Romano Family* series, of which Kiss Me At Midnight is the fifth book. She also authored *The Secret Life of Daydreams* and *One Small Chance*.

Please visit her website at lucindawhitney.com for more information and news.